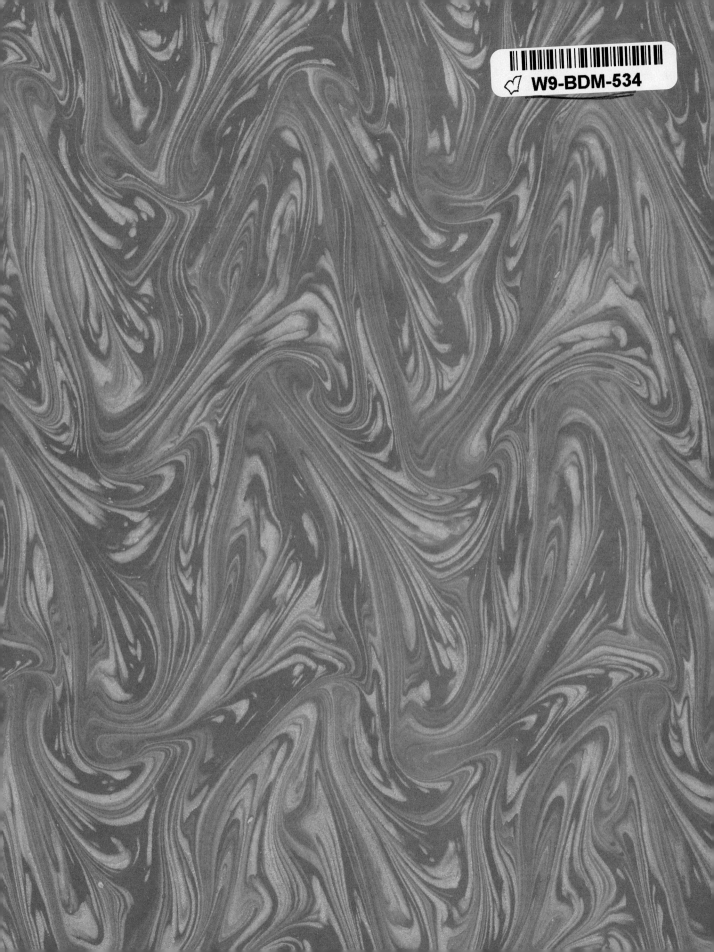
W9-BDM-534

The Newcomers

AUTHORS

Timothy Findley

Guy Fournier

David C. Humphreys

Charles E. Israel

Alice Munro

George Ryga

GENERAL EDITOR

Charles E. Israel

TRANSLATOR OF "THE PASSAGE"

Sheila Fischman

HISTORICAL NOTES

Dennis G. Adair

Janet Rosenstock

CAPTIONS

John Newlove

PHOTOGRAPHERS

Norm Chamberlain

Jean-Pierre Karsenty

Murray Mosher

Dan Mothersill

Richard Pierre

John de Visser

ART DIRECTOR

Frank Newfeld

The Newcomers

Inhabiting a New Land

McClelland and Stewart

The publishers wish to thank Imperial Oil Limited
for the opportunity to publish The Newcomers,
inspired by Imperial's one-hundredth-anniversary
film series, a dramatic tribute to Canada's heritage.
We also wish to acknowledge the assistance of
Nielsen-Ferns International, the company commissioned
by Imperial to produce The Newcomers *series.*

COPYRIGHT

© 1979   McClelland and Stewart Limited

TEXT

The Succession
© Charles E. Israel

The Passage
© Guy Fournier

Island and *A Long Hard Walk*
© Timothy Findley

A Better Place Than Home
© Alice Munro

Visit from the Pension Lady
© George Ryga

Guido
© David C. Humphreys

PHOTOGRAPHS
© Imperial Oil Limited

DESIGN
© Frank Newfeld

ALL RIGHTS RESERVED

ISBN: 0-7710-0158-4

The Canadian Publishers
McClelland and Stewart Limited
25 Hollinger Road, Toronto M4B 3G2

Canadian Cataloguing in Publication Data

Main entry under title:

The Newcomers

ISBN 0-7710-0158-4

1. Canada – Emigration and immigration – Fiction.
2. Canadian fiction (English) – 20th century.*
I. Munro, Alice, 1931-   II. Israel, Charles
E., 1920-

PS8329.N482   C813'.01   C79-094386-7
PR9197.32.N482

PHOTOGRAPHERS

Prologue: Richard Pierre/*1740* and *1847:* Jean-Pierre Karsenty *with* Dan Mothersill/
1832: Norm Chamberlain (CBC) *with* Murray Mosher *and* John de Visser/
1911, 1927, and *1978:* John de Visser

Contents

Foreword

When Imperial Oil decided to mark its one-hundredth anniversary by commissioning a series of motion pictures, The Newcomers, that would celebrate the contribution of immigrants to Canada's social history, it faced a formidable task.

For a start, there was the daunting scope of the subject matter. Even seven hour-long films – the most ambitious project of its kind ever undertaken by private enterprise in Canada – could not hope to offer a large enough canvas to paint anything approaching a complete picture of more than three centuries of settlement. Selection was clearly necessary.

Imperial and the producer of the series, Nielsen-Ferns, decided to focus on those experiences common to all immigrants, regardless of time, nationality, or race, and on those periods in the country's history when those experiences appeared to be most intensely realized. Thus, the underlying themes of immigration – the constants of separation, hardship, domestic conflict, homesickness, the search for freedom, and the crisis of identity – became the criteria for the series. It was also decided to attempt to cover the significant historical periods, each of which presented its own distinctive problems and conditions.

There were other imperatives. To reach as wide an audience as possible, the films had to be suitable for television. They also had to be appropriate for educational use. Both of these conditions required the films to be presented in both English- and French-language versions. They had to be entertaining as well as educational and informative, one reason why the documentary-drama format was chosen. They also had to be historically accurate.

The result was a remarkable partnership between a wide variety of disciplines. To ensure the highest artistic standards some of the country's top writers (including two Governor General's Award winners) were commissioned to write the scripts, and musical scores were written by a number of well-known Canadian composers. Historical accuracy was guaranteed by having all material vetted by a board of eminent historians. Painstaking research was carried out not only to corroborate all historical references but to ensure that every visual aspect of the films, from the re-creation of an Indian village to the small costume details, was faithful to the original. The dramatic portions of the films were produced in both English and French.

The early immigrants to Canada, from the *coureur de bois* to the homesteader for whom, as Leacock wrote, "a plain meal at sunset in a log cabin [was] a very glimpse of paradise," left a heritage on which succeeding generations of newcomers were to build. And they in turn were to become the pioneers for generations of immigrants to come.

It is to all these pioneers that the seven films and this book are dedicated. In today's search for a Canadian identity we all have much to learn from their experiences.

Introduction

Their beginnings, like the origins of many peoples, are indistinct. Some claim they occupied the land forever. Others maintain they reached it through a series of laborious migrations: across the polar ice bridge from Asia, over the stormy North Pacific, up from the tranquil islands of Melanesia.

They were called Beothuk, skilled hunters and fishermen who lived near the shores of the Atlantic and were known for their gentleness. They were named Cree, and surged restlessly across the heartland of the continent. Ottawa, Ojibway, Iroquois – they reflected the character of the regions they settled, and left their distinctive imprint on the land. They were called Nootka, Haida, Kwakiutl, and in the remote mountains and fjords of the west coast they constructed an aggressively materialistic society. They called themselves Inuit, and fashioned rich legend from the art of Arctic survival.

They took from the earth, but they gave back respect. Only after the coming of the white man did they learn to despoil. . . .

The early Scandinavians were renowned for their knowledge of the sea and feared for the way they exercised their skills. During the ninth and tenth centuries they terrorized the coastal cities of Europe, plundering, laying waste. Their boats were small and swift, equipped with sails, and designed for attack. The Scandinavians were reviled as pirates, but they were also a disciplined, sophisticated, and literate people, and in their dealings with each other observed an elaborate code of honour.

To most Europeans of the time, the Atlantic was a mysterious and forbidding ocean. To the Scandinavians, it was merely another portion of a far-flung domain. They had long since established settlements in Greenland, halfway across the stormy northern sea. It was inevitable that they should be the first Europeans to reach North America. In the year 1000, Leif Ericsson led an expedition to Canadian shores.

No one knows exactly why the Norsemen came. It is doubtful they were looking for new lands to conquer. A more likely explanation is that they were an inquisitive and adventurous people – roving was in their blood. Ericsson's party built a settlement, hunted and fished, even cultivated a bit of land. Then, after a few years, they abruptly departed. As far as is known, they never returned.

But they knew of the land to the west. Ericsson's voyage is celebrated in Norse song and legend. If later European explorers could have consulted the Scandinavians, they would have learned that crossing the Atlantic was not the most direct route to the Indies.

Columbus thought he had reached Asian shores in 1492. So did John Cabot, five years later, when he landed on Cape Breton. His illusion persisted as he went on to explore Newfoundland and the Labrador Coast.

Though Cabot was Genoese, he sailed under the patronage of Henry VII, and planted the English flag on the territory he discovered. It was the French, however, under Samuel de Champlain, who established the first more or less permanent settlement in 1603. For a time his community thrived, but Champlain's successors were more interested in exploiting the colony's resources than in sinking roots.

By the middle of the seventeenth century, despite the energetic commerce of fur traders like Pierre Radisson, the French venture in North America was faltering. Then a sudden bold resurgence, imaginative advances to the west and south, gave France huge new holdings.

Still the French people showed little inclination to emigrate to the new land. By contrast, the British had been resolutely settling the continent. Soon they outnumbered the French twenty to one. In addition, they gained control of the sea. Following Wolfe's victory at Quebec, Great Britain took formal possession of Canada in 1763 under the terms of the Treaty of Paris.

In one sense it can be said that Britain consolidated her gains in Canada by massive settlement. Yet immigrants from the British Isles came to the new country largely out of desperation, because their lives were intolerable at home.

The Welsh fled crippling poverty and English oppression, arriving in Canada as early as 1763. The Irish migrated mainly after the failure of a rebellion in 1797, and during brutal famines in 1822 and 1847. The Scots, superb pioneers always, began a steady immigration from the moment the British secured the colony. But even they left Scotland in especially impressive numbers during the political, social, and economic malaise of the 1820's.

The new settlers had great expectations. Naturally, they hoped to improve their material situation. They also believed, even though they were still ruled by the same government, that they would now be free of the suffocating restrictions they had endured in the past.

At first they were disappointed. All the old evils awaited them in the new country. Absentee landlords represented by vicious, thieving agents. Greedy employers. A governing body alternating between cruelty and indifference.

Some of the settlers accepted the new repression as docilely as they had suffered the old, but others resisted. All over the young colony small rebellions against entrenched privilege were fermenting, maturing, succeeding. In the mother country the perpetrators might have been shot or at least jailed. The colonists were aware that the local authorities tacitly condoned the prevalent low-grade larceny. But they gambled that the government possessed neither the vigour nor the effrontery to support flagrant injustice. In most instances the risk paid off, and precedents were established.

The early arrival of another group exerted considerable influence on the fledgling colony. Over 40,000 United Empire Loyalists had opposed the American Revolution and fled the United States after the British defeat. Many were gifted craftsmen and experienced farmers. As they put down new roots throughout the land from the Maritimes to Lake Huron, they at once helped to stabilize and strengthen the communities in which they settled.

Along with them came large groups of Germans who were also out of sympathy with the American Revolution. They were the first significant influx of immigrants who were neither French nor British.

They were welcome. The land cried out for settlers. From the western border of what is today Ontario all the way to the Pacific, vast stretches lay empty, waiting. Gradually they arrived – the restless and adventurous from every continent. The dispossessed. The persecuted.

By far the greatest number came from Europe. Many were either farmers before they left home or became farmers out of necessity. They built crude huts, ploughed and sowed, took off the first meager harvests, cultivated more land a few acres at a time, until the west began to burgeon.

Icelanders, who began communities such as Gimli, "the great hall of Heaven." The Dutch, who introduced strip farming, a major deterrent against soil erosion. Ukrainians, arriving late in the nineteenth century, erecting sturdy sod huts, coaxing plentiful crops from land that was often mediocre. Never forgetting, even after they began to be absorbed into the general population, who they were or where they came from.

The American Civil War flung thousands across the border – black escapees and dislocated whites, forerunners of even larger migrations. In 1912, the promise of free land brought 120,000 Americans to homestead in western Canada.

Nor was farmland the only enticement. In the 1850's gold was discovered in the Cariboo, a mountainous region drained by the Fraser River system. The ensuing rush attracted prospectors of every nationality, including the Chinese. Later, other Chinese would flock to Canada, lured or dragooned into menial labour on the transcontinental railroad, but most of those who plunged into the Cariboo were gold-seekers. More than four hundred Chinese staked and worked their own claims.

For the most part it was an orderly expansion, this westward push. The Canadian Pacific Railway reached the coast by 1885. Finns, Italians, and Swedes were among those who, together with the Chinese labourers, helped complete the east-west link.

It was a peaceful expansion. Canada may have been born in conflict, but unlike the United States, it was not conceived in revolution. The American west grew violently. Canada matured at least in part through orders-in-council.

In 1896, the Laurier government, through its Minister of the Interior, Clifford Sifton, issued a forceful appeal for immigrants. The response was substantial: Swiss, Scandinavians, Russians, Germans, and citizens of the Austro-Hungarian Empire arrived in significant numbers. Most of these, in accordance with the terms of Sifton's offer, settled in the west.

Many came seeking relief from religious oppression in their native lands. Jews fled the pogroms epidemic in Eastern Europe and roamed the countrysides of Manitoba, Saskatchewan, and Alberta, peddling door to door, laying the foundations for solid retail establishments to be presided over by their children.

The Mennonites were perennial migrants. From their original homes in Holland and Switz-

erland they wandered over the course of centuries to Germany and eventually to Ukraine. But by the beginning of the nineteenth century many Mennonite leaders had come to recognize that they would never be free to practise their religion in Europe. In the 1890's, numbers of Mennonites journeyed to North America, joining even larger groups that had emigrated earlier. Some of the new arrivals settled in western Canada, forming exclusive communities where they still speak a dialect of archaic Low German, a language they have kept alive through centuries of transplant.

The Mormons of Utah and Idaho felt discriminated against by the law prohibiting them from having more than one wife. A group left the United States and made new homes in the southwestern corner of Alberta, on the site of the present town of Cardston. It took them less than four years to establish a community store, a cheese factory, a flour mill, and a lumbering operation. They also brought with them sophisticated irrigation techniques which enriched the agricultural production of the region. Ironically, just three years after their flight from the United States, the Central Mormon Church officially relinquished the precept of polygamy.

It would perhaps have been too much to expect – that the peaceful, orderly expansion of a nation could be accomplished without ugly prejudice. True, the demonstrations of bias in this peaceful, orderly country have only infrequently been violent.

However, we did put up signs at the height of the various Irish migrations, "No Dogs or Irish Allowed." We were contemptuous of the Chinese labourer, even as we set him to work at abominable wages building our railroad. We jeered at the Slavs, made snide jokes about the Jews and excluded them from our schools and clubs. We bought goods from the Sikhs who arrived early in this century and peddled for a living. Sometimes we even gave them shelter for a night. But when we did, we often locked them in a barn or shed until morning.

We envied the industrious Hutterite farmers,

whose tight-knit cooperative communities flourished while ours often faltered. We sold them what little they needed, taking their money even as we proposed laws to restrict their prosperity. And we rounded up our Japanese citizens, some from families that had been here for half a century, stripped them of their possessions and sent them to live in icy, sunless valleys as punishment for the crime of ethnic kinship.

Yet, despite imperfections, prejudice, and hardships endured by early and late arrivals, they came to us. And they come to us still.

From every country of Europe. From Asia. From Latin America and the Caribbean. Gladly. Reluctantly. Sometimes considering Canada as only a way-station, a stopover en route to the United States. Then remaining, frequently by accident, or inertia, settling in, slowly and often unconsciously sinking roots.

After they are here for a time, they change. They become more North American, more "Canadian." But they never completely lose what they brought with them. And often the change works in reverse. One has only to recollect the reserved, puritanical Toronto of 1950, before the energetic and joyous invasion of Italians, Greeks, and Portuguese.

The land absorbs but does not homogenize the newcomers. As with our earliest immigrants, those we call "native peoples," each group makes its impact, each individual leaves his mark.

CHARLES E. ISRAEL

The Native Peoples

This hemisphere was once without human habitation. It was a vast wilderness, a volatile land of swift deep rivers, still-growing mountains, great glaciers, and thousands of lakes. This virgin land, rich in plant and animal life, was far from where our human ancestors are thought to have originated.

The history of this hemisphere is one with the history of human migration. The first newcomers are thought to have begun their journey some 30,000 years ago. Evidence suggests they travelled a slow and difficult route across a narrow land bridge from Asia. Their migration eastward was gradual, and the last of these people, who arrived between two and three thousand years ago, are believed to be the ancestors of the Inuit.

The wanderers may have come in familial groups, or they may have travelled as small, closely related communities following game. In the thousands of years before Europeans began their migrations westward, the native peoples travelled to almost every corner of the hemisphere. They developed many cultures, perhaps as many as four hundred languages, and their civilizations ranged from hunters and gatherers to remarkably sophisticated groups, which were in many ways further advanced than their European contemporaries.

In pre-European Canada there were over fifty tribal groups and, while each of their languages was distinct, linguists divide them into five major groups: Hokan-Siuan, Algonquian-Wakashan, Nadene, Penutian, and Eskimo-Aleut. In spite of their great diversity, the native peoples of North America are thought to have numbered only about one and a half million at the time of European discovery.

While each tribal group had a distinctive culture, all had certain common characteristics: religion and medicine were inseparable, oral literature was rich with both religious mythology and familial histories, and government as well as daily life was characterized by long-standing traditions. Hunters, farmers, traders, or artisans, the native peoples, the first newcomers, were one with their environment. They lived on a land that could belong to no man, but which, like the stars of the heavens, was part of a totality – a world to be shared.

Prologue

The Gitksan, whose name means
Skeena River People, have lived
in northern British Columbia
for thousands of years. There
they created a vastly rich and
intricate culture, in which
art and ambition, religion and
ritual were intertwined. There
were both slaves and free men
among them, but an aristocracy
controlled the politically and
socially independent villages.
In each village, a number of
families vied for wealth and
for honour, surrounded by the
marks of Gitksan genius: great
ornamented houses, dramatic
and sophisticated totem poles,
extravagances of dress and
adornment. The figures they
carved and painted with such
skill and care kept alive for
them the power and memory of
their ancestors, their rights,
and their history. These were
not a new people in the land.

The Gitksan inherited both
an enduring tradition and
pride in their accomplishments
and in the sophistication of
their polished civilization.
All the nobles traced their
descent back to the clan's
mythical founder. They were
ambitious for themselves and
for their families. Every
powerful position involved a
title and specific rights:
to sing a certain song, to
hold possessions and wealth,
to carve special symbols, to
dance a particular dance. A
nobleman's successor usually
was a son or nephew; but his
choice must often have been
based on more than family
relationships. Character and
accomplishments would have
mattered also; and struggles
for power and prestige would
have been as unending, as
complex, and as interesting
to the rest of society as
they are to members of
any intricate culture.

The Succession

CHARLES E. ISRAEL

I could hear him behind me. I didn't have to turn to know exactly what he was doing. He would be carrying his bow in a certain way – his grasp on the handle just a little askew to accommodate the stiffness in his knuckles which had lately begun to plague him. I knew the play of muscles in his arms and thighs as he stole along the forest floor, moccasined feet questing, searching out patches of cushioning moss. I was aware of his expression: the sudden fierce puckering of skin around his eyes as he peered through the dense foliage. All of this I knew without once looking around.

It is said among our people that no two men are closer than an uncle and his nephew. Not friends, not brothers, not even father and son. There is a reason. When still an infant, a boy is taken out of his father's house and sent to live with the family of his mother. Seventeen summers ago my mother's oldest brother, Sagagwait, high chief of our village, took the responsibility for my up-bringing.

Behind me I heard a twig snap, then the sharp intake of his breath, a heavy thudding as he sought to regain balance. A year ago this would never have happened. It saddened me each time I

had to recognize a new sign that he was growing old.

He would be ashamed of having made a sound. I quickened my pace, pretending I saw something on the trail ahead.

"Ksaweal . . ."

Something in his voice. I stopped and slowly turned. He was looking at me strangely.

Too often when I was a young boy he knew what I was thinking. I wondered if he could tell now, if he was aware of what had been constantly in my thoughts since the winter before. I hoped not. On reflection I was sure. Otherwise he would not have been smiling so warmly.

"There will be no deer today."

I shook my head and waited for him to catch up.

On our way back to the village my uncle explained in great detail a judgement he had rendered that morning. A gigantic bear had been killed near the fork in the river, and two men each claimed the carcass. Sagagwait had asked for proof. Each man handed my uncle an arrow which he swore had killed the bear. Sagagwait smelled the tip and shaft of each arrow, then awarded the bear to one of the men.

"How did you know?"

"His was the only arrow that smelled of bear fat."

A hooding of his eyes, a twitch at the corners of his mouth. "I believe," I said thoughtfully, "that neither arrow smelled of bear fat."

He stopped walking and laughed until the tears came.

"Shurag is lazy," he said finally. "I never believed he could hunt down a bear."

"You could have been wrong."

"Shurag could have protested."

My uncle put his arm around my shoulders and we walked on in silence. Although he was careful never to speak of it, I knew his greatest wish was for me to succeed him as high chief. He was thinking about it now. I felt his thoughts strongly. They turned the pit of my stomach cold.

It was mid-afternoon when we reached the village. My uncle left me and joined some elders, members of his council who were gossiping outside the feast house.

I took a deep breath and started across the main clearing. Beside a fire two women were butchering a mountain goat and tossing chunks of meat, still oozing blood, into a wooden box filled with water. A third woman picked red-hot stones out of the fire and dropped them into the box. Steam rose as the water began to boil.

It was a sight I had witnessed several times a day for as long as I could remember. Yet I stared at it as if I were seeing it for the first time. And I remained there, because it was the only spot in the clearing where I could stand without being tempted to look towards the cluster of totems in front of the houses. I knew I must not do that.

I heard a voice shout my name. Kselok was approaching with a dozen other young men of our village. They were about to begin a mock-battle, and they wanted me to join them.

Kselok was like a brother. He had been my partner in the bathing ritual. Every morning until their sixteenth year, winter and summer, boys of our village are made to rise before dawn and plunge naked by pairs into an icy stream. When they emerge, old men especially assigned to the task are waiting to whip them with willow switches. The ordeal is intended to fortify our characters.

Kselok was a mimic. Often after the ritual he would imitate the grim expressions of the old men standing beside the stream. Only, however, when we were alone. He would never have dared to belittle law and custom in front of others.

He was grinning at me now as I took my place beside him in the mock-battle. I braced myself and looked across at the enemy. An instant of stillness, then the ferocious outcry as both sides plunged forward.

I found myself grappling with my cousin Gallay. He was older and stronger, and had already demonstrated his prowess in real battle. But I was quicker and more agile. In no time I pinned his arm behind him. I exerted all my strength and forced him slowly towards the ground. Gallay strained, resisting. Sweat blossomed on his body, turning the skin greasy. He began to slide out of my grasp. I held on desperately.

Everyone in the village knew that Gallay wanted very much to be the next high chief. The ambition worked so powerfully within him that often it was visible in his eyes. It glittered there now as we strove face to face, grunting, breathing through clenched teeth. I shifted my weight abruptly, and gained a more secure hold, this time on Gallay's shoulders. My right hand crept along his neck, fingers snaking towards his windpipe. In another moment he would be helpless.

Then I caught a glimpse of the elders grouped around my uncle. It would be their decision, taken soberly in the council house, that would determine who would be the next high chief. They had stopped their conversation and were watching Gallay and me, silently, intently. I knew they thought I was too young for the honour, untried and inexperienced.

I felt Gallay's body tense. I tried to hold him, but my strength suddenly fled. His breath whistled savagely as he flung himself out of my grip. His elbow smashed into my ribs. I gasped with pain.

Then I was lying on the ground, Gallay's face

above me, triumph gleaming in his eyes. I thought I heard the elders sigh, but I might have been mistaken. My side ached excruciatingly each time I drew breath, yet I felt oddly light-hearted. As if I had just received the most lavish of gifts.

Gallay turned from me. I struggled to my feet and found myself looking across the clearing, directly at the totems. They stood stark against the pale sky, the carved animals brooding. At their base sat the girls, dexterously embroidering with quill needles.

She was not among them.

My heart was pounding. I turned back to the mock-battle and plunged to the aid of Kselok, who was fending off two of the enemy. I must finish this, I thought, I must end it quickly.

But it was some time before I was finally free. The sun was beginning to set as I ran into the forest. Through the dark latticework overhead I could see its last rays turning the snowy tip of the mountain crimson.

She was waiting beside the river in the secluded spot where we always met. Hair the colour of onyx, graven perfection of lips, cool beauty of bare shoulders.

But as I approached I hesitated. Her smile of welcome was too bright, too unchanging.

And her voice, high, chirping, like a songbird gone mad. "I don't believe I told you about my dream. No, not one dream. Five. Five different dreams in five nights." Now I perceived the tinge of bitterness in her eyes. "One night I was an eagle, the next a wolf. And then a blackfish, a fireweed, a killer whale."

I took a step towards her. "Neeloak . . ."

"They were beautiful, my dreams. I felt so free."

I reached out to take her by the shoulders, to hold her, stroke the anguish from that fevered voice. She ran from me. I plodded along in pursuit, wanting to catch her, half-wishing I wouldn't.

Every child born among our people is a member of a special kinship group. The child has no choice. Whichever kinship group his mother belongs to becomes his. No one can change his kin-

ship group. And no man can marry a woman from the same kinship group. It is one of the strictest laws of our people.

She slowed in front of me. I gathered her into my arms. Beneath my hands her shoulders rose and fell with her breathing.

"I woke up and knew my dreams were only dreams." Her own voice again. Mournful, almost inaudible, but her own. "I am not an eagle. I'm not a wolf, or a blackfish, or a fireweed, or a killer whale."

She didn't go on. She didn't have to. The words hung all around us beneath the darkening sky. *I am a raven.*

And my reply, also unspoken but persistent as a heartbeat: *I am a raven.*

I had been wondering for some time how long we could avoid discovery. A few nights later we narrowly escaped it.

My uncle was presiding over a minor feast. Minor because the guests were undistinguished: two sub-chiefs from a scraggly downriver village. The gifts they brought were unmemorable – a few crumbling shell necklaces, a tiny mask carved from flawed obsidian – but the courtesies had to be observed. Sagagwait's gifts in return reflected, as was proper, the generosity of a wealthy man. An exquisitely fashioned obsidian knife, an elkskin which looked and felt soft as a cloud.

The main dance that evening was the tale of the invading bear. Two whistles sounded the opening alarm. Then a guard rushed into the firelight to warn that a rampaging bear was heading straight for the feast house. The comings and goings of guards, the rich voice of the singer, and finally the bear, a masked villager cloaked in fur, lumbering into our midst.

Neeloak was sitting on the far side of the feast house. I was seated on my uncle's right, the visitors between us.

I have no idea what made me abandon my usual caution. Perhaps the feast meal I had just eaten, the warmth of the fire, lulling my senses. Perhaps it was the way she looked that evening –

dark eyes wide, muted firelight lending her hair an enchanting gloss.

I was staring at her. Openly. I knew passion was blazing in my eyes. I made no effort to conceal it.

And I was thinking. Imagining. Planning? I would stock a canoe with food. There would have to be enough to last us all the way to the sea. We could not risk hunting or fishing, nor would we be able to stop at any villages. The chiefs, fearing my uncle's displeasure, would surely have us taken prisoner and sent back to receive our punishment. We would travel by night, slipping downstream between heavily forested banks, resting by day, until we finally reached the shores of the Great Ocean.

We would find a hospitable village whose people had no ties with ours, who would accept without question a young man eager to serve them as warrior, hunter, fisherman, even a tiller of the soil. Where none would know or care that the young man and his bride were both born ravens.

A chunky woman representing a whirlpool seized the intruding bear and enclosed him in a capacious embrace as she circled the floor of the feast house.

Neeloak must have felt my gaze. She was looking at me now. I was sure I would never be able to turn away from what I saw in her eyes.

The two whistles shrilled again, signifying the rout of the bear and the close of the dance. Somehow the sound penetrated our trance. Neeloak first. I saw her lips, parted with desire, twist then compress as she wrenched her gaze away.

Her fear became mine. I turned swiftly toward my uncle. He was staring in my direction. Then he glanced at Neeloak. Impassively, eyes unrevealing.

I was certain that Sagagwait had seen what passed between Neeloak and me. But he did not speak about it that evening, nor in the days that followed. Gradually I became convinced he had noticed nothing.

The summer was passing. I continued to meet Neeloak in secret whenever I could. There were moments when we would forget who we were and be happy for a time. But more often knowledge came between us, even when we were in each other's arms.

One morning early, Kselok and I went out to fish. The air was crisp, the sun rising bravely, free of cloud. A jay rebuked us without pause all the way to the river. High above, a raven executed a long, lazy spiral in the still air.

We passed two women spreading fish to dry on racks. The riverbank was steep here, and soft shale made the footing treacherous, but we knew it was the best spot for salmon. We used our spears to help us down the sheer slope.

Just downstream the water ran white, and the sound made talk impossible. I motioned for Kselok to stay where he was. I would go a little upstream. I started away, then glanced back and saw a flash of silver and gold in the sunlight. Kselok had already impaled a large salmon and was grinning as he flipped it up on to the shore. A good beginning.

I'm not sure exactly what happened then. I was just beginning to fish, wading out into the shallows, spear poised, waiting, watching, when the cry came. At first I thought it might be the jay still scolding or the women on the bank calling to each other, but then, above the sound of the rapids, I heard it again.

I saw him. Bobbing in the water, flailing, struggling against the vicious current. He must have pursued a fish too far into deeper water and missed his footing.

He was losing his battle with the river. Another few moments and he would be sucked into the rapids. One of my cousins had died in that white fury. No bone in his body had remained unbroken. I splashed through the shallows, keeping close to the bank, never taking my eyes off Kselok.

He clutched at a rock. The surface was smooth and slippery, but somehow he managed to hold on. It was a forlorn respite. He was already tired.

Soon the water would tear him from his refuge. I felt grief.

Then anger. The river would not rob me of my friend. I strode out into the water.

I brought him in. It wasn't easy. At least twice as I worked my way from rock to rock I was certain the river would claim two victims. But I brought him in. We lay exhausted on the bank, grinning wanly at each other.

Word of the rescue spread swiftly through the village. It was the kind of deed our people esteemed. Their praise made me uneasy. I repeated over and over that I had only done what anyone would do. That made it worse. They assumed I was being modest, and modesty is an attribute our people prize nearly as much as courage. I noticed that some of the elders were regarding me with new respect.

It was then I knew I had to speak to Neeloak. That night. If I waited I would never do it. The prospect made me reckless.

When I thought everyone was asleep I crept through the house where she was quartered with her sisters and cousins. Her obese old aunt acted as chaperone. A young girl's virtue was a precious commodity, to be used for bargaining at the time of marriage, never to be squandered mindlessly before.

I lay beside Neeloak's pallet and watched her sleep for a time. Then I woke her, as gently as I could, but not gently enough to keep her from crying out. The aunt snorted loudly and began to mutter, but after a moment the house was once again silent.

I whispered to Neeloak about the canoe, about my plans for flight, about what we would find once we arrived at our sanctuary on the shores of the Great Ocean. I told her we would leave as soon as I was able to gather provisions. A matter of two days, no more. She listened without replying, frightened, but I was confident I could override her fears. I held her close for an instant. The old aunt began to snore as I stole out of the house.

The next morning I began to collect food: dried fish and meat, berries. I would also have liked to take along some valuables for trading – obsidian, a skin or two, perhaps even a small box of oolichan oil – but as yet I owned little of importance, and I would die before I would steal from my uncle. No matter. We would be together. We would survive. In time I would amass wealth.

On the morning of the second day following my visit to Neeloak, a report reached our village that intruders were fishing in waters belonging to Sagagwait. We had to investigate – my uncle, Gallay, I, and enough others to fill three war canoes.

The report turned out to be false, but the foray consumed two days – two precious days of my new life with Neeloak.

Upon our return, we beached the canoes in the placid backwater below the village. My uncle immediately left us and started up the trail. He was of course exempt from the chores performed at the end of a patrol. Impatiently I carried out my assigned task of seeing that the canoes were well out of the water and secured. I left Gallay and the others to collect the weapons and provisions. I hurried into the forest. What I saw after I had taken only a few steps chilled me.

My uncle was lying motionless in the middle of the trail. At first I thought he might be dead, but then I heard him moan. I knelt beside him, took hold of his shoulders and began to drag him off the trail. Weakness displayed before others is humiliating to any man. For a high chief it meant disgrace. I pulled him into the concealment of a tiny glade.

None too soon. I could hear the others coming along the trail. My uncle was recovering. He smiled his appreciation to me for protecting his reputation.

He began to talk. I had known he wanted me to succeed him as high chief. Until that moment I hadn't known how much.

He stopped speaking. His face was drawn with pain. Death lay in his eyes, waiting. In the silence a raven cawed from a branch above our heads. I had not realized it was there. The bird flapped its wings and rose from its perch, clumsily at first, grace and assurance increasing as it reached the open sky. My uncle watched the raven until it vanished, then motioned for us to go.

That afternoon I resumed preparations for the journey I would take with Neeloak. As I worked – collecting supplies, carrying them secretly to the canoe hidden beneath closely laced brush – I savoured the knowledge that by the time the sun had risen and set twice more, we would be alone together on the dark waters of the river. But some of the joy had fled from anticipation. I could not blot out the earlier events of the day: my uncle's expression, his voice warm, stern, wistful by turns.

Therefore I was not overly surprised by what took place that night.

The evening began quietly. A group gathered in my uncle's house to sing and laugh. Not a feast; there were no guests. Family, villagers, relaxed, convivial, as we almost always were when no strangers were present to impose formality. An ordinary evening, no warning, not even a hint of danger.

I slipped away as soon as I could. The air was unexpectedly warm. The moon laid down a shimmering path into the forest. Mist rose off the river, dark patches catching a swift hint of silver before retreating among the trees.

Where Neeloak was waiting we could still hear the voices from my uncle's house, rising in song. She had been combing her hair. Gently, I took the comb from her. She glanced at me, and when I moved towards her, she drew away. Among our people a woman's hair is one of her most precious possessions. Combing it is a highly personal ritual, the woman's act of reassuring herself that she alone is in control of her spirit. To allow another to comb her hair is considered an invasion, at the very least, surrender.

I persisted. Neeloak drew away again, this time turning to look deeply into my eyes, her expression puzzled, pleading. What she saw there must have made her understand, for suddenly she sat quite still. I raised the comb once more. I

felt the trust flow between us. The last barrier had vanished. We began to laugh.

Then we heard the voice. A low chant, gathering intensity, freezing our laughter, stilling the song from my uncle's house, finally ringing in mournful, solitary splendour through the black reaches of the forest.

We all knew the voice. It belonged to the *halaait*, the medicine man of our village. He was singing to warn us of disaster. He did not know what the calamity was, or who would be affected. All he was certain of was that it would happen soon.

And I was sure the *halaait*'s warning was meant for one person alone.

I could not let him see my concern, for that would have been disrespectful. Yet I tried as much as I could never to let him out of my sight. If I could not prevent harm coming to him, I could at least be there when it happened.

And for the moment there could be no further thought of leaving the village. Only after my uncle's death, after I had mourned his departure with both ceremony and love, would I be free to begin my new life with Neeloak. She understood.

It hurt me to watch Sagagwait now. I saw him in conversation with the elders, and I thought about the spirit of illness working within his body, and I remembered the day when I was no more than four or five and he threw me up into a blaze of sunlight and, our laughter ringing, caught me as I fell.

One afternoon I followed him to the riverbank where he inspected and praised a new smokehouse. As he turned to climb back up the hill, I saw the deep lines in his face and understood finally what it would be like never to see him again, never to hear that soft and patient voice.

And as I watched, and wept inside, and recalled him striding through the forest as a young man, my vision abruptly shattered into a thousand brilliant fragments, then grew dim, and faded entirely as a roar of sound engulfed me. My knees were buckling. Wild darkness and the sharp shameful realization that I had lost control of my bowels and bladder.

I refused to believe. Darkness, darkness and disbelief. A scream, high-pitched, bereft . . . triumphant? Neeloak, or a demon drunk with conquest lurching forward to claim his prize.

For me. The *halaait*'s warning was meant for me.

I lay in darkness and knew the approach of evil. I followed its progress up from the black fires of the netherworld. I watched it lurk faceless at the rim of the clearing, willing noon to become nightfall. I sensed it gliding toward me through the shadows. I felt my own spirit flee. I heard its soundless cry.

I lay in darkness, yet all was clear around me. I heard the chant of the *halaait*, the harsh twitter of the rattles. I was aware of the erratic firelight, the sheen of sweat on the *halaait*'s forehead, the blank and fearful stare of his assistant.

I lay in darkness and I knew all because I was dying. Soon my spirit, already departed, would summon my body, and they would be joined forever in some restless void beyond the mountain peaks.

I would hear them mourn – those who loved me and those who merely respected my death. I would listen to the crackle of flame as it devoured the criss-crossed logs of my funeral pyre. And I would feel no regret, for my death was forecast, ordained, and therefore correct.

I heard the voice of the *halaait* now, hoarse with fatigue, exhorting. I felt the gentlest of breezes and knew he was wafting the divining feather the length of my body, searching for the evil he must cast out. I felt he would not succeed. My eyes were closed and I could not move.

My eyes were closed, but I could see Neeloak standing outside the house in the shadow of a totem. I could hear her breathing, I could feel her fear.

I saw an arrow penetrate a man's throat. I saw the rose and purple guts snake out of a huge hole in a deer's side and strangle a child. I saw a woman's head split in two by a blow from a war axe. I heard all the sounds of pain and terror.

I saw my uncle's face, and in the calmness of his eyes I lost my fear. I lay in peace, listening to the rise and fall of the *halaait*'s chant. Darkness descended. This then was death. Darkness and silence. I lay in peace.

But the darkness shifted and roiled, and once again I knew anguish. The *halaait*'s voice battered at my ears. The darkness shaped itself into a raven's head. Its scream blended with the words of the *halaait*. I wanted to cry out. I could make no sound.

Then I felt my eyelids flutter. The *halaait*'s face was close to mine. A smudge of soot streaked his left cheek. His eyes were rimmed with red. But he was smiling.

He helped me sit up. I felt strength flow back into my limbs. The *halaait* cleared his throat. Even so, when he spoke his voice rasped.

"You will eat?"

It was more command than question. I nodded. He stood, not moving, waiting.

"I will eat," I said finally.

And suddenly, as I spoke, I was aware of the meaning of my life, what it had always meant, what I would have known long before if I had only been capable of understanding.

I knew now. The sickness had taught me. The darkness gave me light.

I stood up, took my first step, and almost fell. The *halaait*'s assistant sprang to help me, then stopped, warned by a glance from his master.

I walked to the door and stood looking out at the faces thronging the clearing. My uncle's smile was jubilant. Kselok laughed aloud. I turned my head slowly, responding to the greetings, the cries of relief. I did not see her anywhere.

I knew where she would be. I did not keep her waiting, I could not.

Her voice was scarcely more than a whisper. "Ksaweal . . ."

I knew she was not pleading. I would not have expected it of her. I wanted to take her in my arms. I knew I would not. The forest lay calm around us, expectant. I began to speak. "In the darkness . . ."

"No," she said. She shook her head slowly, then got up from the rock where she was sitting and walked away. I did not try to stop her, but long after she was gone I continued to stare at the spot where she had disappeared among the trees.

Fate never follows a straight path. Decision is always edged with irony. Now I wanted the council to choose me. Now I wanted my uncle's authority to pass to me when he died. I wished to take the name Sagagwait. Now I was ready to pledge my strength and my life to the people, and in return I wanted the respect, obedience, and tribute they would owe me as high chief.

The morning after I met Neeloak in the forest I scoured the high reaches beyond the village, hoping to catch sight of a mountain goat. A high chief must be a bold and skilful hunter. If I could return with the carcass of one of these nimblest of creatures, my reputation would begin to grow.

It turned out to be a useless morning. The sun was just crossing its zenith as I returned empty-handed to the village. I entered the clearing and stopped. People had abandoned their chores and were clustered about something, shouting and gesticulating. On the other side of the clearing Sagagwait and some elders emerged from the house where the council had been meeting. Curious, they advanced towards the knot of people, which separated at their approach.

What I saw then turned me sour with envy. A man, grimy and bedraggled, hands tied behind him. And standing beside the prisoner, spear in hand, my cousin Gallay, basking in the appreciation of the villagers.

He saw me and crossed the clearing, leaving to others the relating of his prowess to the elders. It was a clever move. He could appear modest before the council and at the same time enjoy the pleasure of watching my reaction as he told me about his adventure.

Early that morning when Gallay was crossing one of the hunting preserves belonging to our uncle, he saw the stranger who now stood shackled in the clearing. Since the man carried a spear, Gallay suspected he was planning to hunt on Sagagwait's land. He followed, and when he saw the man kill a doe, he attacked and overcame him.

"Now, of course," Gallay concluded, with exactly the right mixture of condescension and self-satisfaction, "our uncle can either demand ransom from the fellow's family, or keep him as a slave."

I did not hate Gallay. Not at all. He was my cousin and I had affection for him. Only at that moment I could not bear the sight of him. But I had to admit he had acted boldly. It was the kind of deed our people admire.

Nor was my mood improved when I listened to the elders heaping praise on Gallay as he rejoined them. My uncle glanced in my direction and looked away at once. Not quickly enough. I felt his disappointment like a blow.

Courtesy demanded that I stay in the village for the remainder of the afternoon and join in the accolades for Gallay. By sunset I had had enough. I slipped away to the beach below the village and set off across the backwater in a small canoe. I dug my paddle into the still water, delighting in the way the tranquil reflection of sky splintered and grew chaotic. All excellence, I decided, taking another vicious stroke, is just this vulnerable and temporary.

I thought I heard someone call my name. He was standing on the shore, his back to the scarlet sky, tall and imperious. Now, I thought, he will tell me how unhappy he is that I have not been able to match Gallay's achievement. Sagagwait called again. I hung back. I did not feel I needed to be reminded of my inadequacies.

My uncle beckoned. I dared not delay longer. I directed the canoe in toward the bank and took exceptional care beaching it so I would not have to look at my uncle's face.

"I understand what it meant for you to give her up."

I turned, startled, not sure I had heard correctly. The lines around his mouth were set and austere, but there was a great gentleness in his eyes. He put his arm around my shoulders and we stood in silence. The sun vanished from the sky. Darkness had begun to blur my uncle's features when he spoke again, so softly I almost missed his words. "It is the sign of maturity I have been hoping for."

The day hovered between summer and autumn. The night before was cold, and just after dawn a few snowflakes had drifted out of a bleak sky. The afternoon, however, was warm, the air in the forest still and oppressive. Thunder muttered as Kselok and I set out to hunt.

"Perhaps . . ." Kselok began, then stopped as he looked at my face. I knew what he had intended to say. I would not turn back, not until the rain actually began to fall. Often in the moments just before a storm animals lose their caution. I had become an obsessive hunter. Already I had brought several mountain goats and two large black bears into the village. I was determined to continue until I achieved renown. Once, I would not have hunted without my dear friend. Now it no longer mattered whether Kselok accompanied me into the forest.

Something stirred among the ferns ahead of us. I fitted an arrow into my bow and advanced slowly towards the curtain of foliage. The sound of thunder was louder now and more frequent.

Kselok gasped, and I saw the raven – the huge beak, the luminous, malevolent eye peering out of the gloom – only for a moment before it vanished.

Evil comes in many forms. Sometimes it may take the shape of an animal or a bird, sometimes even the kinship animal of the person it confronts. Occasionally it can resemble a human being. Rarely, it appears as some combination of man and beast.

Kselok and I looked at each other, then pressed forward warily. The trail led upward now, almost obscured by dense undergrowth.

The raven was waiting for us at the edge of a glade, watching us intently, half-concealed behind the trunk of a giant tree. Lightning flashed, and in the pause between the radiance and the crash of thunder, the raven screamed.

Kselok's face hung open-mouthed for an instant against the dark green of the forest. Then he was gone, and when I turned again, the raven had also disappeared.

I was frightened. I would have been content to hurry after Kselok and return with him to the village. Somewhere in the depths of the forest an enormous creature was waiting, watching for me. There was no reason for me to pursue or provoke it.

None except Gallay and the advantage he still held over me.

The sound of thunder was almost constant now, drums challenging and mocking one another from a ring of mountain peaks. I moved up the trail.

It grew steeper. I had to climb over a succession of rotting logs. Ferns and creepers clutched at my legs.

I thought I saw it – an iridescence of black and white feathers gleaming in the strange light, a menace of yellow beak, the grim and implacable eye. Yet I was not certain, for I thought I saw it lunge away on human legs.

I fought my way clear of the forest to a bare patch of mountainside and looked around. The raven was nowhere in sight. There was only one place it could have gone. I took a step, then another, towards the cave which opened between two massive segments of rock. I strained to see into the blackness. Lightning flickered. From the mouth of the cave the way led downward. I could determine no more than that.

I was certain by now that the demon which threatened me during my illness had returned in the guise of a raven and enticed me here to reclaim my life. If so, it would do no good to flee. He would only try again. I had to confront him now. I had to vanquish him.

A couple of steps past the entrance of the cave there was a sharp drop-off, so steep that I had to use both hands to ease myself down the rocky incline. No doubt he had counted on this, had contrived it so I would have no opportunity to use my weapons.

I reached the floor of the cave. Far above me I

could make out the entrance. The light it admitted was meager. I could see nothing.

I took a step. My foot encountered something solid. Round.

Lightning. And in the flash I saw that my moccasin was resting against a man's skull. Beyond that another, this one attached to a complete skeleton. My heart pounded. I gripped my bow, knowing even as I did that it would provide no defence. I waited, preparing to fend off the slashing beak, the tearing claws.

Lightning. I let myself relax in the darkness which followed. There was no raven.

There *were* two enormous shields, lying on the cave floor a few steps from the bones of the men.

I sat in the chair of honour in the feast house, watching the play of firelight across the burnished surfaces of the shields, listening to the singer relate how I took possession of them. Seldom had I seen my uncle more pleased. Among our people there are few possessions more highly prized than copper shields. He had summoned many people, even representatives from several of the downriver villages. He had lavished food and expensive gifts on the guests. He wished to be sure that all would remember this feast, and why it took place.

Neeloak was sitting among the women just beyond the circle of firelight. It was not easy to see her face. I was grateful. I knew what would come next.

I did not, however, expect it to happen so soon. A scant ten days after the feast, I was surprised to see the canoe carrying the three strangers approach. The man in the centre of the canoe was splendidly dressed and self-important. He had a mannerism – pursing his lips and wrinkling his nose at the same time – which made it appear that for him life was a perpetual foul odour. His expression did not alter once as he surveyed the beautiful objects set out on the beach for his appraisal: richly dressed elkskins, exquisite obsidian, five huge boxes of precious oolichan oil.

He had come to bargain and he was good at his job. The bride who had been chosen for me would not be purchased cheaply.

I heard singing. It was difficult to tell where she was. The mournful voice seemed to float from everywhere at once – the river, the mountains, the clump of bushes behind the feast house.

I found her in the forest. I saw her before she saw me. She had stopped singing and was shuffling along the trail, head bowed, forlorn. The madness took hold of me.

She looked up as I raced past her, grasping her hand, pulling her along with me. There might have been joy in her eyes. Certainly there was excitement. There was no surprise.

I had removed the provisions, but the canoe still lay under the concealing brush. Perhaps I had known this would happen. Perhaps I had hoped for it.

Reluctantly I released her hand. She helped me strip the ferns and branches away from the canoe. I held the tiny craft steady while she stepped into it. I thought about the nights we would spend together on our journey to the sea. I thought about how it would be to waken slowly and know she was beside me. I thought about the years ahead of us: the passion, the tranquillity, our children, our love.

Her smile was tremulous as she waited. I glanced across the water. No one. I took hold of the gunwales and began to ease the canoe away from the bank.

At first I thought it was someone who had rushed down the trail in furious pursuit. The cry was shrill, compelling, venomous. Then I saw Neeloak looking up towards the overhanging branch.

The raven.

The murmur of the river, the rustling of the trees, the slow drumbeat of flapping wings as the bird rose and circled above our heads.

Once I had crept close to the clustered totems and listened as the old aunt rehearsed the girls under her charge in the lore and laws of our people. That morning they were discussing marriage, and I had smiled as I heard Neeloak's voice rising in recitation: "When a bride drinks for the first time after the wedding, she must rotate her cup four times in the direction the sun moves."

I watched my new wife turn the cup. I saw her drink.

"Then they will be happy for the rest of their lives."

My wife smiled up at me. The wedding song began. My uncle, transported with happiness, nodded his head in time with the music.

"The wedding guests shall try as hard as they can to make the bride and groom laugh. If the couple can manage not to laugh, it is another omen for their happiness."

Kselok was cavorting in front of me, giving his imitation of a bear. I had seen it often. Always I had found it hilarious. I glanced at my wife. We smothered our laughter.

I did not see my uncle. I looked around, searching among the faces in the feast house. He was not there.

We found him among the trees. He had not wanted the others to witness his shame. He had not wished to disrupt the festivities. He saw me running towards him and died calling my name.

Women poured water upon flames, extinguishing every fire in the village. Men blackened their faces with soot. Children sat listlessly in brilliant sunlight.

These are the signs of mourning.

A measured voice began to chant the melody of loss and regret.

These are the signs of grief.

The raven drifted out of the white sky, circled once above the treetops before settling on a corner of the feast house roof.

It rained that night, a prolonged downpour which dwindled only with the onset of dawn. They built the funeral pyre with wood they had sheltered from the rain.

We watched them stacking the logs, Gallay on one side of the clearing, I on the other, as we waited.

Finally the elders came. They stood between us, for the moment looking neither to right nor left. A ritual posture. Both Gallay and I knew by now the choice they would make.

I accepted the carved staff. As I did, they brought the torch to the pyre. Before the mounting flames I pledged my final allegiance to my uncle and to my future.

I knew she was standing near the main trail where it curved before it entered the clearing.

I turned from her, even as I knew she had begun to walk away from the village into the forest.

The French

Spain and Portugal were the first European nations to explore and conquer new lands. In search of a shorter route to Asia, they found America; and rather than Asian wealth, they found the wealth of Mexico and Peru. These discoveries and the return of the Portuguese explorer Magellan spurred both the French and the English to send out expeditions.

Jacques Cartier headed not for the southern part of the hemisphere, but for the northern part previously explored by Giovanni da Verrazano. Cartier did not find gold and silver, but he did find native peoples willing to trade furs. He laid claim to the area where New France was to be established, but it was not until 1603 that Samuel de Champlain founded the first permanent colony at Tadoussac.

Some historians believe that the beginning of the fur trade was the most important event in our economic history. Unhappily, conditions both in Europe and in North America limited the success of France in the New World, and although the colony of New France prospered, it was also plagued by war and, on occasion, famine.

The French allied themselves with the first native peoples they encountered, the Algonquin, who were incidentally at war with the recently formed, but powerful, Iroquois nation. The English, who established colonies farther south, soon allied themselves with the Iroquois. As a result, wars that developed between the English and French in Europe spread easily to the New World, fed by tribal animosities.

Many of the French who came to New France did so to escape a feudal system that limited land ownership. Others, of course, came simply in search of adventure and wealth. Few French, however, were willing to emigrate in spite of the many incentives offered by the French Crown. Unfortunate Indian alliances, little settlement at the critical period of colonization, and disastrous defeats in European wars all tended to discourage French expansion in North America. By the 1750's there were less than 50,000 colonists in New France, while there were 1,500,000 settlers in British North America. Even so, the French coureurs de bois and their Indian wives were the vanguard of westward movement. They created a new race, the Métis, who by the late 1800's are said to have numbered over 60,000 in the west.

Today, nearly all French Canadians trace their ancestry to the original settlers who arrived between 1665 and 1739. One of Canada's founding nations, the French helped to change the face of the land and its people.

1740

From France to an alien world

New France was founded on a class structure that originated in Europe. The culture of seventeenth-century France set the standards of the time. Her language and social patterns were transplanted to the new colony, but before long a system and style more suited to the new land began to evolve as New France expanded.

The faces of New France

Those who came to New France sought a society in which a person could move from one social class to another – a freedom denied them in France. Their lives were also changed by the severe climate and the cultures they encountered. The people were changed and changing, and traditions adapted to the strange and vibrant land.

Life was not only different, but beyond the carefully guarded confines of the settlements and farms, it was also dangerous and precarious.

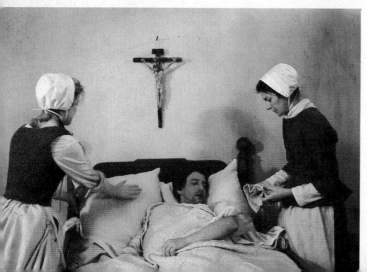

The *habitants,* as the French settlers were called, farmed land owned by the *seigneurs,* who encouraged settlement by offering to give land and money to any man who married and raised a family in New France.

Working together
and using
the materials
available to them,
the *habitants*
established homes
and families.
Self-sufficiency
became a way of
life for the people
who now called
themselves *Canadiens*.

The desire for money and position spurred much of the expansion and discovery in Canada in the early years. But the way was strenuous and severely tested those who took it.

Help was sometimes available from the Indians and the more experienced *coureurs de bois,* but the journeys were often arduous and the means of transport primitive.

Perils and profit

When disaster struck on the trail or in outlying
settlements, help was rarely close at hand.
Even if the journey was completed safely, the
outcome could be disastrous or profitable
depending on luck and the fur market in Europe.

The profits to be gained from fur-trading were great, but depended on the demand for pelts. The beaver trapped by a *coureur de bois* might ultimately become the hat of a fashionable Parisian.

The austere beauty of the land
belied its abundance, exacting new skills and
new ways of thought in exchange for survival.
For those who took up its challenge, it yielded its
riches and shared the ageless mystery of its spirit.

The Passage

GUY FOURNIER
translated by SHEILA FISCHMAN

Cautiously, Catherine unfolded the scrap of newspaper. It was marked with brownish lines and fragile as a dried leaf. Sensing that she was being watched, she performed each motion with unusual grace. As she unfolded the bit of paper, she raised the ring and little fingers of her right hand, as a highborn lady might do. This sudden affectation was not lost on Nicolas, who bit his lip to force back a smile. Catherine's self-consciousness was not wholly unflattering, and he continued to stare at her which only increased her awkwardness. As she had been taught at the Ursuline convent, she coughed slightly to avoid the squeaky voice that always threatens a young woman about to read aloud, and began to recite the news from *The Gazette:* "'Monsieur Théophraste Renaudot, beloved founder of *The Gazette* and former physician and secretary to the King, graced with his presence the dazzling party given by our dear Marquise de Tençin in her salon. In his capacity as Commissioner General responsible for the poor, Monsieur Renaudot took advantage of the glittering occasion to read a message of hope for our less-favoured brothers, which *The Gazette* will publish in its next edition.'"

Before going on, Catherine looked up to make sure Nicolas was still following her. He smiled.

She turned back to her paper: "'Jeannette Antoinette Poisson, daughter of the renowned financier, caught the attention of everyone present when she arrived at the party in a carriage so richly ornamented that the King himself might have taken umbra—'

"There's no more," said Catherine apologetically, as though she herself had been responsible for cutting off the page.

Catherine explained that a distant cousin had sent her from France a pair of elegant shoes wrapped in this scrap of newspaper, shoes so beautiful she had decided to keep them for her wedding day. She had also kept the newspaper that talked about marquises and princesses and carriages, which she could see now as clearly as if she had been at Madame de Tençin's party.

"What are you thinking of?" she asked, sensing that Nicolas' attention had strayed.

"My country," he replied.

"I shouldn't have read the newspaper to you."

"Oh, but I would have thought about it all the same, Mademoiselle Catherine."

Then she, too, became pensive. She paced nervously, speaking of her father, who was to become the *seigneur* of Neuville, of the sheep in the fold, the wool to be spun, the partridges to be shot; but what did it all matter compared with the vineyards of Touraine where Nicolas de Lugny was born, or the fine houses in Bourgeuil and Vouvray or the Château of Chinon? Catherine, whom the nuns had taught resignation and humility along with arithmetic and reading, lowered her head. She had no right to divert from his chosen path this young cadet who had come to New France to win the officer's stripes it would have taken him years to earn if he had not consented to this exile.

Nicolas then described the towers of the Saint-Gatien cathedral that were fifty *toises* high and built of massive stones, monuments carved from top to bottom that would stand for hundreds of years.

"Amen!" thundered Louis Gagnon, stamping his foot on the doorstep both to clean the mud off his thick leather boots and to announce his presence. "Enough of this twaddle. It's time to go to sleep!"

He gestured to his mother-in-law who was dozing with one eye and watching her granddaughter with the other; then, without apology, he stepped over Nicolas' outstretched legs and, with one breath, extinguished the three candles Catherine had placed on the table near her.

"I'm off to see the Intendant in Quebec tomorrow. You will accompany me, du Lugny."

Without further delay, he stomped into a small bedroom and climbed down a three-runged ladder that no one had ever remembered to attach to the foundation of the house. Catherine's eyes were so misty she didn't notice that, as her father spoke, Nicolas had removed the sheepskin that had covered his legs, and left. With the sheepskin under his arm he went directly to the guest room, which was connected to the sitting room by a door concealed under the stairs.

How long did Catherine remain there motionless? The fire, which had been high in the fireplace, died completely before she resigned herself to go upstairs. And though she walked lightly so as not to attract attention, Nicolas heard her go. He longed to call her name, but was unable to utter it aloud.

Never had a young woman made him feel so awkward. He worried about the most insignificant details: his breath, his somewhat moth-eaten wig, his dirty fingernails, even his voice, which he pitched lower when he spoke to her! What did it mean? He finally fell asleep without finding an answer.

When Catherine heard the whinnying of the horses her brother François was harnessing for the journey to Quebec, she was still wide awake. The burning sensation she had felt in her chest when she first uncovered the face of the man she had pulled out of the river more dead than alive, had grown more acute with time; nor had it deceived her, although she was only sixteen. She was in love, and she knew it. Her grandmother knew it, too, and had prayed in vain that Catherine would not see the two men leave. But love is not so blind, and when Mater – as the old lady was known to everyone – went to bolt the door that François had left open, she noticed Catherine at her window, the first light of dawn silhouetting her figure against the muslin curtains.

"Now dry those tears," said Mater when she saw Catherine's red eyes. "Fancy, letting yourself become so upset over a passing stranger, and a soldier at that! Tomorrow he'll be in Quebec, next month in Detroit, and then in France or Santo Domingo. There's no shortage of men; at your age if you lose one, two more turn up to make you forget him."

In Quebec City, Nicolas de Lugny, agleted cadet of His Majesty, was poorly received indeed. Because he had been unable to recapture the two villains who had plunged him into the St Lawrence River with one firm stroke of a paddle, he was assigned to stand guard at the palace of Intendant Hocquart. He would not win his stripes there!

Louis Gagnon, who had made a great point of telling de Lugny in what high esteem he was held in Quebec, was received no better. The Intendant, whom he had just beseeched to accord him the title of *seigneur*, with all attendant rights, privileges, and honours, was in a bad mood, and ill inclined to listen to this wily Norman who also wanted a fur-trading permit to pay the expenses of a flour mill, a survey of his estates, and cleared land for a parish, as the local gentry was required to provide.

"You're all blinded by fur," Monsieur Hocquart exclaimed, grinding his teeth and cracking his knuckles, so hard was it for him to contain himself. "You think the beaver is the only resource of this country!"

Every high official has his little whims. Monsieur Hocquart's was to transform the economy of New France. No more of this fur nonsense! The future lay in fishing and shipyards; there was a crying need for ships to harvest cod in the gulf, as the Spanish, the Portuguese and the Basques from the other end of the world were doing.

"In Paris," Gagnon protested obsequiously, "people have interest – and money – only for furs."

Had he known the Intendant better he would have avoided the very word "fur," which caused Hocquart to spring to his feet once more.

With both fists on his desk, Hocquart deigned to point out that if he had fur-trading permits to distribute he would give them to military men, who were becoming dangerously soft as a result of an idle peace that had gone on too long. To emphasize his determination he pounded the table with both fists at once.

Gagnon could only retreat. He took refuge at an inn run by a man named Nolan, to whom he had always been able to release his pent-up feelings as he drank rum and nibbled lumps of sugar, all the while berating the cursed Frenchmen who had come to lord it over everyone in Canada. Monsieur Hocquart's ears must have been burning that night, for neither Nolan nor Gagnon suppressed their outrage at this man who would devour the common people, who tried to find a place both in the King's chamber and in the good graces of the devout. The two cronies came close to unleashing a revolution half a century before it was due.

The unexpected arrival of Nicolas sealed Gagnon's lips. He winked at Nolan to let him know that if the wretched Intendant had thwarted his most legitimate plans, then Providence was coming to his aid in the person of this officer.

"So then, de Lugny, you've come to drown your troubles away at my friend Nolan's, too, have you?" he asked cockily.

Astounded to see Gagnon hold out his hand and smile, Nicolas stammered that he was simply here for a simple game of cards with his companions from the barracks.

"A round for the soldiers," Gagnon ordered loudly, then told Nicolas quietly that he wanted to speak to him privately.

The soldiers' coarse laughter, which Nolan's cheap wine encouraged, prevented Gagnon from being overheard as he set his snares for Nicolas. Gagnon was crafty enough to know that the smaller the stakes the more generous the speech must be. In the offhand manner of one not at all concerned, he explained that the Intendant was in a most regrettable position: he would provoke the anger of the envious if he were to award Gagnon a fur-trading permit along with the title of *seigneur*. On the other hand, the Intendant needed wood for his shipyard and could not afford to disappoint Gagnon, whose lands were covered with good wood for building ships. Gagnon clicked his tongue and nervously stroked his chin to show Nicolas how cruel the Intendant's dilemma was. Nicolas would have liked to display some sympathy, but knew virtually nothing about politics. As a supreme gesture of his confidence in the young man, Gagnon murmured to him the very words of the King's representative: "Monsieur Gagnon, find an officer to whom I might give a fur-trading permit, who would then cede it back to you. In that way I shan't depart from my principles."

"An officer? Why an officer?"

Not only did he have to draw a picture for this beardless youth, he had to colour it in, too!

"See here, de Lugny, this is quite normal. In peace time, you must keep up the morale of the troops, especially when the soldiers' pay doesn't arrive very regularly."

"Have you found the man you need?" Nicolas asked, trying to comprehend.

"With the coin of the realm everything is possible – though that's not my general principle."

Gagnon sighed, with honeyed words, that he was looking for an ambitious, upright man who might wish to contribute to the possible birth of a *seigneury* – in a word, a man like Nicolas.

"Me? You ascribe so many virtues to me?"

"Be careful now," Gagnon went on, as though he had not noticed the young man's surprise. "You must be discreet, silent as the grave. As Monsieur l'Intendant himself suggested, 'Your name must never be uttered, Monsieur Gagnon, not even before me. If it were, public opinion would tear us to shreds.' So, de Lugny, what do you think?"

There are times when a man risks choking on his own saliva. Flabbergasted, Nicolas stammered that he knew nothing about fur-trading.

Gagnon laughed heartily, relieving the tension. "But you needn't even get your feet wet! Simply obtain the permit and I'll buy it back for twice what you paid. The idea is to act fast enough to snap up the finest pelts from under the noses of the traders who'll wait for spring."

It was Gagnon's turn to come close to choking as he watched Nicolas first turn pale with indignation at such underhanded dealings, and then exclaim with pride that if he obtained a permit he would do the trading himself. He was about to get up, but Gagnon plucked at his sleeve.

"Listen, de Lugny, are you so rich that the crowns I'm offering you are of no interest?"

"My only interest is to get back to France as quickly as I can – with a full commission."

"Penniless?" Gagnon asked bitingly. And sniggering, he pulled on a thread that was dangling from Nicolas' worn tunic.

"By the power vested in me by the King, by the grace of His Excellency the Governor General of New France, Sieur Charles de la Boische de Beauharnois, I declare that this trading expedition has been verified before witnesses in the presence of Olivier Quatresous, captain of the militia, and in accordance with the edicts, orders, and mandates of our government. May God help you!"

With a militia man who trembled like a frightened bird by his side, the captain clumsily delivered his harangue in a thundering voice as though he were addressing an entire army, then came to shake the hand of the leader of the expedition, Nicolas de Lugny, whose rather pale complexion and effete manner betrayed the fact that he was a cadet – and brought mischievous smiles to the lips of the two men it was his mission to command. The four Indians who rounded out the expedition seemed far too dazed to differentiate between a true *coureur de bois* and a chocolate soldier.

"A trading expedition in the middle of winter? They aren't out of the woods," Captain Quatresous said aloud in a sententious voice, as he saw the men lugging toboggans loaded with barrels of lard, axe-handles, rakes, and the rest of the gear they would trade for furs in the *pays d'en haut*.

Grasping his purple nose between thumb and forefinger, he blew his nose and tossed a thick gob of snot in Nicolas' direction. "On top of everything they've got a washed-out young whippersnapper leading them who's probably never been on snowshoes in his life!"

Although it was frequently said that Captain Quatresous couldn't find his own fingers once he'd stuck them in his pockets, he nevertheless discerned the expedition leader's ingenuousness. It may be said in defence of the captain's detractors, however, that this lack of guile was as plain as the nose on his face: while Cotenoir and Pinot La Perle, doubled up with laughter, were pulling the biggest toboggan, and the Indians were harnessed to the other two, Nicolas led the way, marching as though on parade. At this speed he had soon outdistanced his troops, which made him think that his army training made him more skilful at leading a fur-trading expedition than were the colonists, whose reputation for lack of discipline had long ago reached the mother country. No one in France was surprised since colonists were all black sheep who had been lured by promises of the rich grazing lands awaiting them on the other side of the ocean.

Although Gagnon had never admitted to Nicolas that Cotenoir was his own most trusted man, he hadn't concealed the man's good qualities either. He had said just enough about Cotenoir to let it be known that he had great esteem for the fellow, who was solid as a pine chest and had even travelled around the world.

"He's been to China?" Nicolas had asked, his eyes as round as gold coins.

Gagnon had lowered his voice and his head as he gave an affirmative reply: "You could count on one hand the people who have actually seen Chinamen up close and lived to tell the tale!"

Pinot La Perle was a total ignoramus. For him, the south meant La Pérade, the north Tadoussac. As for east and west, he had seen no more than he could take in at one glance. He had the instinct – and the loyalty – of a hunting dog; and one was never quite sure whether his loyalty lay with his master or the victim he held in his teeth. Cotenoir knew this and gave him no more rope than necessary. He used him to scour the countryside, to drive out game, and to laugh a little. For despite the fog in his brain, Pinot would on occasion come out with flashes of wit, which always succeeded just when Cotenoir was about to lose patience; and for this gift the former adventurer forgave him much.

After walking for several days across the hard-packed snow on the path overhanging the St Lawrence from Montmorency to Baie Saint-Paul, the travellers had to take to the woods in order to reach Chicoutimi without needless detours. As soon as the expedition left the heights where the open wind steadily swept the snow, the pace slowed to that of a snail, hindered further by Nicolas' refusal to put on snowshoes. He used them instead to beat at the snowdrifts it make walking easier, explaining that rather than struggle against the snow one should let oneself be carried along by it, like a keel on the open sea. Cotenoir suggested to the nominal leader that he

follow behind the caravan so that the heavy toboggans and the snowshoes of the men pulling them could pack down the snow. Nicolas allowed himself to be overtaken, then left behind.

"They got thick noggins, those Frenchmen, eh, Cotenoir?"

As though Cotenoir weren't French himself! He shrugged, glanced behind him, and quickened his pace. Gagnon, the real boss, would get an earful for having stuck him with this little runt. Cotenoir was willing to write off the whole wretched matter: Pinot's idiocies, the Indians' nonchalance, the crass ignorance of the officials, and even Gagnon's pettiness; but the reasons of state Gagnon had invoked for imposing de Lugny on him still stuck in his throat. Frustrated, he spat into the snow and was preparing to do so a second time when Pinot called out to him.

"Whoa, Cotenoir! The flagship's just run aground!" Pinot stood in the open air slapping his hands against his thighs like a seal.

"Whereabouts?"

"Don't know," Pinot replied, feigning great sorrow. "The Indian told me he hadn't seen him since the crooked stream. Think we should recite the De Profundis?"

Pinot's ripple of indecent laughter ended in a question mark when he saw the look on Cotenoir's face.

Cotenoir found de Lugny in a far worse state than he had imagined. Clinging with blue fingers to a root and standing to his waist in a torrent that cascaded down from a height of three or four *toises*, Nicolas dared not move for fear the root would give way. He was well past the De Profundis and into the Act of Contrition when Cotenoir's broad hand clutched his collar. With his other hand grasping a small maple tree, Cotenoir lifted the unfortunate man as nimbly as though he were using a capstan. Nicolas' snowshoes lay at the bottom of the waterfall, toes up.

"There's others," said Cotenoir as he slipped on his snowshoes.

Numb and exhausted, Nicolas, whose cold wet trousers seemed to be burning his legs, held out his hand to Cotenoir to thank him; but the other man had already turned his back. Nicolas muttered a few thank you's that fell short of their target: with long strides, Cotenoir was heading back to join the caravan. True brotherhood, like great pain, is silent.

When Nicolas caught up with the procession, he decided that they had travelled far enough, that here, in the middle of nowhere and at the mercy of the four winds, they would spend the night. Neither Cotenoir nor Pinot protested. Without consulting each other they set out in search of fresh meat. When they returned with a spitful of rabbits, the fire was burning briskly and a shelter of fir boughs had been erected. After seeing to it that Nicolas had noted that the rabbits had not been eviscerated, Pinot, with the assistance of an Indian, began to turn the creatures slowly over the fire. The rabbits' blood-streaked coats, placed too close to the flames, gave off an acrid odour. Nicolas retched, then moved away from the fire, which was just beginning to thaw his buttocks. When he saw the Indians extract the steaming entrails with the tips of their knives, then eat them with squeals of pleasure, he vomited into the snow.

"Well, well," Cotenoir remarked, looking pitilessly at Nicolas, "it seems that rabbit isn't our leader's strong point."

"Maybe the bunny isn't cooked enough," La Perle opined, spitting out a tuft of fur he had inadvertently bitten off.

"Unless you drink blood and eat guts you'll be a puny runt all your life, eh, Pinot?"

"That's the honest truth."

Pinot, grinning from ear to ear, turned towards Nicolas, who thought he could see the man's own entrails beyond his gaping maw guarded by two yellow fangs. To Nicolas, already feverish, it seemed as if the man had barked.

The next day, de Lugny walked on snowshoes, and despite Pinot's dark predictions, his pace was good, his stride increasingly elastic. Cotenoir, who had spent a busy morning dragging him along, discovered with some pleasure that he had a gift for passing on his knowledge. Nicolas advanced all the more boldly because he no

longer had any idea where he was going: he saw his fellow travellers as though the sun were shining behind them, and the spruce trees seemed to press against him until he felt suffocated. The following day he coughed his lungs out with each stride and staggered like a drunkard. Cotenoir looked at him with growing concern. He had seen too many men die not to recognize death, no matter how it was disguised.

"Halt!" he exclaimed suddenly in his stentorian voice.

Everyone stopped except Nicolas, who rolled his eyes in a threatening manner and muttered between his teeth.

"Who is in command here, Cotenoir?" he asked. Hoarsely, he gave the order to begin marching again.

For Pinot, who had been taught strict obedience, such a situation was intolerable. His distress was short-lived, however, for one half-point of a league further on, Nicolas crumpled into the snow like a sack. This time, Pinot made no foolish remark. Mouth agape, panic-stricken, he looked from Nicolas to Cotenoir, who alone could deal with any eventuality, even that of burying a corpse. Cotenoir rushed the soldier, grabbed him with both hands and stretched him out on the toboggan laden with blankets of scarlet wool.

"Is he dead?" Pinot asked, crossing himself.

Cotenoir did not bother to reply.

"Fasten him down, you Indians, and don't waste any time. We're going to head for the coast; we're bound to run into some colonists."

Pinot was horrified at the idea of taking such a detour because of a cursed Frenchman who would give up the ghost along the way.

"Rot and botheration! It's Madame La Perle who'll be grumbling when her husband hasn't shown up by Pentecost. I'll be losing her if I have to keep chasing through these woods like a pagan."

His moans had no effect on the decision. That evening, under the direction of Cotenoir, who was overseeing the smallest details, the Indians and Pinot prepared for the sick man a bed that would make a bride envious. On a thick layer of pine needles – tender young ones for the most part – they had spread three scarlet wool blankets and arranged fir boughs all around for protection.

"Why not hang some lace on it, too?" Pinot asked contemptuously.

Nature took over. While everyone was asleep – except for Cotenoir who thought it prudent not to let the fire go out – a gentle snowfall softened the night and even ornamented the fir branches. To keep from dropping off to sleep, Cotenoir began to speak aloud. He explained to Nicolas, who stared at him with glassy eyes, how he had ended up in this strange country from which he could not now tear himself away.

"Funny thing, M'sieu Nicolas, a country like this gets under your skin; the longer you're here the more it grows on you. Take me, now. I never thought I'd be spending the rest of my life here, but now, I don't know."

Not speaking to anyone in particular, he set out to recount the long detour that brought him finally to New France.

One April morning – it was Easter Monday – he had set sail from Nantes for Cape Verde, hoping to reach the Cape of Good Hope, which he had heard described as heaven on earth. But instead of sensibly dropping anchor in this paradise, he had let himself be tempted by a Dutchman, and he was taken on for a voyage to Ceylon. They were to bring back tea for the English in Boston, whose love of their King and four o'clock tea resisted all the vulgar fashions of the new world. The captain had guaranteed the return voyage would be a simple one: after months of battling monsoons and the treacherous channels in the Indian Ocean, the vessel missed tiny Ascension Island and ran aground in the port of Fernando Noronha, a week off the coast of Brazil. The tepid equatorial sea spray destroyed half the cargo, while scurvy wiped out half the crew. Never had Cotenoir thrown so many corpses into the sea. He rebelled against the Dutchman, who should have stayed on the canals of Amsterdam, and decided to wait for a good sailor who took the shortest routes – from the Antilles to Cape Fini-

stère or Guinea, for example. The nationality of the ship mattered little.

"To tell you the truth, M'sieu Nicolas, I was even ready to work a pirate ship. When you're young you aren't too fussy about your travelling companions."

He bit his lip thinking about what he had just said. He approached Nicolas, close enough to touch him, then took up his story again.

At Noronha, he had time to learn Portuguese before signing on as cook on a galleon from Rio that was sailing for Santo Domingo. There they would take on a cargo of Negroes from Guinea, brought there by the French, whom King Louis XIII had authorized to become slave-traders on condition that they did not bring their slaves into the French capital. After chaining the Negroes in the hold, Cotenoir, touched by grace, abandoned ship to settle in Louisiana with his compatriots. He had time to learn Spanish before embarking on a commercial store-ship laden with sugar and rum, chartered by one Nolan, from Quebec. And so it was by these roundabout routes that Elie Cotenoir, six and one-half feet tall, strong as a bull, and speaking three languages, found himself in the bosom of the future *seigneur* Gagnon, with whom he drank rum from the Antilles at Nolan's inn.

His account had been told like the litanies of holy days, sprinkled with Spanish and Portuguese. Nicolas, thinking he was hearing Latin, imagined in his delirium that Saint Peter was hesitating about receiving him into Heaven, while devils in coarse woollen jerkins were dragging him down to Hell.

"Avast! Avast! Aaahh! You rogues, you won't have my skin! Away from here! Help! Help!"

Cotenoir shook Nicolas briskly, turned him over, and slapped him hard on the back, for the young man was turning blue before his very eyes because he was unable to spit out the blood filling his mouth. At length he expelled it but began to sweat from every pore. Cotenoir was appalled. When a man past forty sees a young whippersnapper who could be his own son slip through his fingers, it turns his stomach.

Cotenoir placed his hand on Nicolas' brow the better to moor him to life, and in a falsetto voice began to sing a song he had often thrown to the open wind.

"Je pars pour un voyage
Sur la belle "Etoile du nord,"
Avec mon équipage
Qui s'ra mon réconfort.
Il faut hisser les voiles,
Grand Dieu, quel triste sort!
Priez, priez pour moi, la belle,
Que je revienne au port."

De Lugny could no longer cough or even move under the sailor's hand, which was heavy as a lead weight. Convinced of the therapeutic virtues of his refrain, Cotenoir took it up again, more softly now.

"Quand tu s'ras dans ces îles,
Amant bien éloigné,
Tu trouveras des filles
Qui sauront te charmer.
Et moi, la malheureuse,
Serai la délaissé.
O! qu'l'amour est trompeuse
Lorsqu'on est éloigné."

The last line dropped off, for Cotenoir was falling asleep. Exhausted, he let his head fall onto Nicolas' chest. The sick man was breathing more slowly now and the fire gradually died as the night closed in around them.

"Ugh! It stinks of burnt meat," Pinot exclaimed, burying his nose in the sleeve of his tunic.

Cotenoir sniffed at a bit of air as broad as his hand and could only confirm the verdict. Troubles never come singly. Didn't they have enough on their hands with a man suffering from pneumonia? Cotenoir gestured to the Indians to remain behind while he and Pinot went to reconnoitre the source of the disgusting smell.

Rifles pointed like muzzles, the two *coureurs*

de bois hurtled down a snow-covered gorge at the bottom of which they saw a wooden house surrounded by smoking ruins. The flames had come so close they had burned part of the walls.

"Holy Mother of God! Is it possible the barbarians have burned some poor Christians, Cotenoir?"

The latter motioned to his companion to be silent. Cocking their rifles and taking off their snowshoes, they crept to the door of the house. It opened abruptly when Cotenoir stood up to shoulder it in. Hens and sheep came running out, pursued by a skinny boy who cried in horror when he saw the two men. He retreated inside, calling his father. With broad smiles, Cotenoir and Pinot approached the colonist who came out, rifle at the ready.

"French?"

"French!" replied Cotenoir.

The colonist dropped his weapon and burst into tears in the arms of Cotenoir, who was quite nonplussed.

"Go fetch the crew, Pinot."

The Indians remained some distance from the house because of the stench. Cotenoir and Pinot would have liked to do the same, but the colonist, Boissard, objected. The single room of the Boissards' house held an army: the little boy who had run after the sheep, a three-month-old baby, a small girl just beginning to walk, another just starting to talk, Boissard's wife Zoé, her sister Barbe Daniau, and Barbe's husband who was suffering like a holy martyr. The barn and Daniau's house had just been razed by fire and in his attempts to save his animals – three pigs, two cows, a few sheep and some hens – Daniau had burned both arms. The fire had singed his eyebrows and part of the hair on his head.

Nicolas and Daniau were placed side by side on a broad mattress. Gangrene had already started to eat away at Daniau's arm and the fire had ravaged his entire body. He was moaning like a lost soul.

"Yesterday he wasn't even suffering. He helped us get the sheep and hens out and throw snow on the fire."

Zoé agreed with her husband, but suggested

that most likely her brother-in-law had still been suffering from shock.

"Then his nerves just let go," she said. "It's like Barbe's milk. The shock made it clot so now it won't come out."

Zoé also diagnosed Nicolas' acute pneumonia and, after placing her hand on his brow and her ear against his chest, concluded that only prayer could save him. Cotenoir, who believed more in the Indians than in the Good Lord, decided to entrust the dying men to them. After all, there was nothing to lose!

The eldest of the Abenakis was assigned to care for the half-dead men. Beneath the horrified eyes of the whole household, he began by bleeding Nicolas: baring his arm to the elbow, he held the skin taut by pressing firmly on it with both thumbs while another Indian jabbed a fish-hook into a vein, and immediately withdrew it. Blood spurted out until the wizard wound a tourniquet around the sick man's shoulder. Nicolas, who had scarcely groaned during the operation, now fainted and was stiff as a corpse when they laid him back on the mattress.

"If you ask me they've finished him off," Pinot whispered trembling like a girl at the thought of spending a single moment under the same roof with a dead man.

The Indians removed the outside layer of bark from a pine tree. Then with the tips of their knives, they did the same for the layer beneath it, which they cut into narrow strips. As serious as popes, they chewed the strips for a long time, then crushed them in a mortar until they had produced a smooth paste, which they spread over Daniau's burns. The paste hardened into a plaster, and Daniau had trouble moving his arms in their sheaths of healing salve.

Within twenty-four hours Nicolas' fever had dropped, but he was very weak from the diet the Indians had prescribed for him: nothing but teas brewed from herbs and roots until the next full moon. It was out of the question to resume their journey until he could nourish himself with something more than these concoctions (which, according to Pinot, were as useful as dog piss).

Pinot would have fed him salt pork until he became sicker than ever!

Nicolas decided that his men should help the colonists rebuild the house and barn. Cotenoir didn't take much persuading: he had all the time in the world and these good people hadn't yet heard the stories of his voyages.

Pinot was more restive. "I was all ready to sign up for a trading expedition that might last two or three months, but now if we have to turn into carpenters on top of everything else, I'm raising anchor, as Cotenoir would say."

"If you want to leave," said Nicolas firmly, "you know the way. But the rest of us won't go until these colonists are sailing again, as Cotenoir would say!"

In his heart of hearts Pinot was formulating curses that would make the devil dance, but he sharpened his axe and cut down more trees than anyone else. Nicolas, too weak to work, wrote to his mother. The letter would be added to the others, which were in Quebec waiting for the first ship to France.

Chère Maman, I do not know if it is the fever, but I feel as though my hand has not held a pen for an eternity. I am at the end of the world, my dear mother, far from the worries that our late father's porcelain business must be causing you. After an attack of pneumonia that caught me completely unawares, I am recuperating at the house of some colonists who have been summoned for me from Cap à l'Aigle, a hamlet consisting of a few shacks high above the St Lawrence River. We came here just after the place had been devastated by fire, and a man who was severely burned is slowly recovering, thanks to the Indians who are acting as our hired men. They know a great deal about witchcraft and possess remedies we know nothing about. They heal burns by applying an ointment made from the bark of a young pine tree. The colonists, who preferred not to settle within the shelter of a seigneury, live in complete isolation. This solitude make them extremely hospitable and it is in order to thank them for what they have done for us that we are helping them get re-established after the dreadful ordeal they've endured. Tell my brother and sister that, although I was so afraid of the winter here, it has become almost bearable. The cold in this country is biting, but it's calm and, in my opinion, more pleasant than our own. I, who used to be afraid of a single flake of snow, now swoon with delight at the sight of entire mountains of it.

"The frame's up now, M'sieu Nicolas. I think we should raise anchor."

Nicolas smiled at Cotenoir who stood in the doorway of the shack. Behind the sailor, he could catch a glimpse of the big square beams rising against the sky.

"It's as solid as our leader." Smiling, Cotenoir clamped his hand on Nicolas' shoulder, all the time looking at the letter with curiosity.

"You'll have all the time in the world to finish it, M'sieu Nicolas; we'll be knocking about pretty well till spring breakup."

Since they had been with the colonists, Nicolas felt that Cotenoir had shrunk, that he was now no more than a head taller than Nicolas. The impression continued to grow during the rest of the journey.

In Chicoutimi, at the Ilets Jérémie, and even at Sept-Iles where they had to negotiate nose to nose with the Papinachois Indians, it was the soldier who conducted all business, leaving it to Cotenoir to raise or lower the price according to circumstances. They both worked wonders and obtained in exchange for their gear more furs than the craftiest *coureurs de bois* might have done.

Pinot, who had for so long been Cotenoir's peer, took umbrage at the situation. At Sept-Iles they met an Indian woman, Katéri Pigarouiche, pregnant by a *coureur de bois* from La Pérade, and Pinot took it into his head to bring her back to Quebec with him.

"It'd be an act of charity to bring her back to her man."

He took care to plead his cause to Nicolas while Cotenoir was busy elsewhere. When the latter had remarked that the expedition would hardly be enriched by a pregnant woman, Pinot said curtly that she would be no burden.

Finally, Nicolas announced, "I'm in charge, Cotenoir. We're going to bring her back to her husband, and Pinot will look after her."

"That's all we need!"

One night when everyone seemed sound asleep, Pinot slipped from his pine-needle mattress. Crafty as a Sioux, he crept to the Indian woman's shelter, stopping once or twice to be sure he had not awakened anyone. Without a sound he lay down in her bed, and the woman's eyes gleamed with pleasure. Then they froze in horror when a hand plucked Pinot from the bed and sent him rolling into the snow.

Nicolas clutched the man by the throat, lowering his head until he could smell Pinot's fetid breath, then sent him back to his own mattress.

"A poor defenceless girl," said Nicolas, releasing his grip.

Pinot spat contemptuously, and Cotenoir, who had seen everything, pretended to be fast asleep. He didn't want to take sides. The woods, he thought, are like a ship: never bring a woman on board unless you want a mutiny!

Next morning, Nicolas was the first to awaken.

"Great God! Cotenoir, Pinot, wake up!"

The two men woke with a start and saw Nicolas shouldering his rifle, as he shouted. "The furs, *sacrebleu*! Hurry!"

Rubbing his eyes, Cotenoir saw that Katéri and one of the Abenaki had disappeared with a toboggan laden with pelts.

"Don't be too hard on yourself, M'sieu Nicolas. They're far away by now."

Stunned, Nicolas looked at Cotenoir, who remained impassive, then at Pinot, who lowered his head. There was nothing to be done. Slumping on his bed in frustration, Nicolas inadvertently pressed the trigger of his rifle and a shot rang out, splitting the air. Cotenoir and Pinot began to laugh. Nicolas, too, almost deafened by the noise, chortled heartily.

In the end it was Gagnon who suffered the loss. After going over the accounts with Nicolas, he could only sigh over the meagre profit he would realize.

"When I think that merchants in France will be making a small fortune from our furs without lifting a finger. Canadians are dying while the French are pocketing—"

"In that case," said de Lugny with a hint of a smile, "you might say there's some French sweat in it, too."

"You must have changed if I've forgotten you're a Frenchman!"

Nicolas could not help thinking that only a few months earlier such a remark would have made his blood rise.

Gagnon invited him to dinner, but Nicolas declined, explaining that in his absence the captain had decided to continue Nicolas' service in Martinique, along with six other officers of the company.

"Well, let me congratulate you. You can't be too sad to be leaving us."

Seeing Nicolas' face cloud over, Gagnon put his hand on his shoulder and squeezed it affectionately. For the first time, the young man felt that Gagnon, too, could be straightforward and frank.

"You should go and say hello to Catherine. She's gathering mussels at the foot of the cliff."

Nicolas took his leave. He mounted his horse and headed north; half a league further he turned in the direction of the St Lawrence. He remained at the top of the cliff for a long time, watching Catherine. Her skirt was pulled up to her knees and fastened around her thighs by a length of hemp; holding a basket over her arm, she was plunging her hand into the cold water to gather the mussels. The tide was low and Nicolas was surprised at the dimensions of the beach. It had seemed tiny to him the previous autumn when Catherine had pulled him from the water. If she had not been there, he would never have escaped death. Merely thinking about it made him shudder.

"Yoohoo!"

The wind was in his face, so Catherine did not hear him shout. He remounted his horse and spurred it on without taking his eyes off Catherine. When he lost sight of her, his horse was at full gallop.

Quand tu s'ras dans ces îles,
Amant bien éloigné,
Tu trouveras des filles . . .
Et moi, la malheureuse,
Serai la délaissé . . .

He stopped his horse. Where the devil had he learned that song? The animal pawed the ground impatiently and set off again – at a walk. At this rate he wouldn't reach Quebec before dawn.

Louis Nicolas de Lugny never left for the islands. He did not even leave New France. By the autumn, when his mother received, along with all the others, the letter he had written during his trading expedition, he had already married Marie-Catherine, daughter of Louis-Joseph Gagnon, who still did not have the title of *seigneur*.

The Scots

The colonies of British North America were made up of peoples from the United Kingdom: England, Scotland, Wales, and Ireland. From the beginning, the adventurous, restless Scots were everywhere. It is said that some of the seamen on the early Viking explorations of Vineland were Scots, and that Scots who had emigrated to France were among the French settlers who came to New France. Indeed, Abraham Martin de l'Ecossais, after whom the Plains of Abraham were named, is said to have been a Scot.

Scottish immigration to Canada increased greatly in the eighteenth and nineteenth centuries. Some Scots were driven from their homeland when the Highlands were depopulated so that the land could be used for grazing sheep; others came to escape religious and political persecution, and still others came in search of jobs and cheap land. In addition, a large number of Scots were among the United Empire Loyalists who came to Canada after the American Revolution.

It is difficult to simplify the reasons for Scottish emigration because, unlike many newcomers, the Scots did not come to Canada in distinct waves of immigration or for a single reason. In the 1800's, however, the industrial revolution and urbanization resulted in heavy Scottish emigration to Canada. The rapid increase of population in many cities made housing overcrowded, working conditions intolerable, and unemployment high.

By 1824 workers had begun to organize, but unions, as such, were illegal, and urban workers could not vote. In Scotland, particularly in industrial towns such as Glasgow and Paisley, the struggles of the workers led to riots. The severity with which the workers' discontent was suppressed, together with high unemployment, caused many Scots to emigrate to Canada.

Most of the Scots who came to Canada fell into one of three equally important groups: highly educated, skilled graduates of universities; workers who had the benefit of experience in Scotland's mills, factories, and mines; and the Highlanders, who had earned their livelihood farming and raising cattle and sheep.

Our first Prime Minister was a Scot; Sir Sanford Fleming gave us standard time and helped engineer the railroad west. Many of our trade unions and many of our giant industries were founded by Scots. From the l'Ecossais and the Langlois to the Macdonalds and the McDougals, the Scots newcomers made a tremendous impact on the institutions and traditions of Canada.

1832

When John Symons came to Canada there were few opportunities for highly specialized tradesmen, and certainly none for silk-weavers. Desperate for independence, he found employment cutting trees. Symons later wrote: "The constant clutching of the axe affected the sinews of my hands, which were unused to such a strain, and the fingers remained bent for the rest of my life."

*Unable to practise
their trades, immigrants
were often forced
to take menial jobs*

Many itinerant workers and their
families were hired to make potash.
It was a laborious process:
First the trees had to be cut down
and burned. The ashes were
then mixed with water and boiled
until all the liquid had evaporated.
What remained in the bottom
of the large cauldrons was potash,
which was a very valuable and
essential commodity in the early
North American colonies as
an ingredient in the manufacture of
soap and fine glass. It was
also used to wash the lanolin and
dirt from fleece before it
could be carded and spun into wool.

"After the New Year some time, my friends made a bee and drove out to my lot . . . the trees were soon falling, being shaped into logs, and placed one upon another, so that before it got dark, my shanty was complete. No sawed lumber was used, the floor and the roof being split basswood logs. They left me in possession of it, and I was emphatically alone, for there was no soul nearer me than five miles. In fact the land had not been surveyed. It was solid woods or swamp in every direction."

Without help from neighbours, many settlers would not have survived the many hardships of the early years

After the first lean years,
more land was cleared and cultivated,
better houses were built, and
families left behind in Scotland were
brought over. John Symons recorded
in his diary: "I wrote to
my wife to join me, and went
to work, chopping day after day . . .
in order to have a decent home
ready for her and the children, never
resting until Saturday afternoon."

Wealth and the signs of wealth multiplied, simple but reassuring in their grace and practicality

John Symons made this world his world. Once the task of conquering the land was complete, he had the time and money to surround himself with fine examples of the security and stability a man's estate could grow to, if only one worked long enough and hard enough. But there was more than a moral lesson to be found in his success.

These beautiful objects were crafted with love and care and were as characteristic of the new land as were the people who made them. The Scots' love of books and learning also flowered. When Symons finally prospered he used his wealth and position to further the cause of universal education in years to come.

Island

TIMOTHY FINDLEY

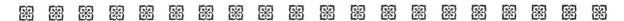

He left early one morning in April, crossing through storms to the other side of the river. He rode the ferry in the company of seven men, three with horses, one with a wagon. Because he had no notion of the distance he would have to go, he envied the men their horses. Maybe, though, he'd only have to walk ten miles or so before he found a job. He let the rain squalls beat against his face. The rain was warm; it smelled of trees. He smiled.

He was an emigrant no more. The leaving was over, and the pain of his wife's last embrace was fading into the pleasure of the thought that one day she would join him here in the Canadas. Now all would be advents. Arrivals. Somewhere there would be a city or a village or a town where he could settle and from which he would send back the message, "*Margaret. Come. There is a house and I have work.*"

Under the wagon children and a woman were hiding from the storm. Symons thought, my children will be born here. Every one. He asked the woman, "Where are you coming from? Where are you going?" And the woman said, "*Je ne parle pas anglais,*" and turned away to shield her daughter from the rain. This was something Symons had

forgotten. Language. Back in Montreal he could subsist on English. Here in the country, he would have to work in a foreign tongue. The prospect alarmed him. Still, another language was nothing compared to the bayonets and bullets he had left behind in Scotland. Or the prison he evaded by coming to Lower Canada. The fact was, Symons' arrival in North America was no mere act of immigration. It was a desperate escape.

The Canadas shone like a beacon in the dark for men of Symons' persuasion, whose integrity was affronted by the prospect of being enslaved by machines and factories and the men who owned them. He was young and something of a firebrand. His craft was weaving, but his trade was anarchy. During the Paisley riots of 1826, which his father had instigated, John Symons became so adept at storming the barricades that his name was placed on a list of "dangerous and desperate men." After the English militia had crossed the border and put down the workers' revolt, he was forced to hide for many weeks to avoid capture and imprisonment. His father had been murdered along with several others – including women and children – and every hope of dignity and decent conditions was abandoned at their graveside. The mills had been re-opened and the workers – some as young as six and seven – had been herded back to the looms. All at the point of the bayonet and under threat of starvation.

John Symons knew then he must seek asylum somewhere beyond the limits of this terrible conscription. But emigrant Scots, particularly when they came from Paisley, could not afford to journey south through a hostile England to Plymouth and Bristol from where the ships for America sailed. The better chance was to take a ship from Clydebank and get to Canada.

What Symons found, when he got to Montreal in April of 1827, was a city of foreigners, most French, but many English. He was treated with neither courtesy nor meanness, only indifference. And perhaps with an edge of wariness. People debarking from ships were invariably suspect: their clothes might be vermin-ridden and their very touch and breath might communicate disease. Plagues of cholera and typhus swept the provinces from end to end, wiping out families and even whole communities. The chance of finding a decent job was almost nil, unless one had been arranged before leaving home. The only work to be had was degrading and dispiriting: burying the dead, digging latrines, or killing rats, the traditional work of lepers and drunkards.

So he had to make a choice: stay in the city and compete for the worst jobs, or venture into the country and find what he could on the land. It was the latter he chose.

A man he had already heard speaking English was standing to the lee of the horses as they neared the shore.

"I know," he said to this man, "there's towns out there along the river and farms, too, as far as that goes. But aside from them, the charts they show you and the maps I seen got nothing much but a blank the whole way out to the Pacific. What *is* there?"

The man was squinting at the rain, but he turned to Symons and gave him a strangely unnerving smile. "Trees," he said. "Just trees. The bastards."

It was a prophetic statement. Trees were to govern Symon's fate for years to come – and perhaps for life.

He struck out alone with everything he owned on his back. Space alarmed him. He was used to the confines of crumbling walls and narrow streets. The road that ran along the St Lawrence, with its meagre commerce of carts and horsemen, gave him a prospect of lowlands suitable for farming but which, nonetheless, seemed sparsely populated. In the distance he could see the forest – but he never quite reached it. Always the road veered away, avoiding the trees, meandering instead through the meadows and in and out of flooded fields where he had to walk through water up to his knees.

For the first six days of his journey, he paid for his food out of pocket. The cost was just pennies; the fare was mostly farmers' cheese and bread and, on occasion, cups of cider. But he knew he could not afford this luxury for long. His wealth amounted to a five-pound note and a leather bag, the size of his fist, containing his coins. These were mostly gleanings from his sisters' dowries, given as he bade them farewell. The gifts were to be the foundation of a fortune.

The spring rains continued. He slept in barns, although he would have preferred the fields, away from the dogs. But all the haystacks had been depleted by winter, and the woods were filled with bears. Or so he imagined. Bears and wolves were the stuff of legends told about this land at home. Not a creature existed in the North American bestiary of his imagination that did not eat men. Even the squirrels and rabbits haunted his dreams in scenes of carnivorous abandon. The dogs, however much he feared them, were at least echoes of the dogs at home. And mice were mice no matter where they were encountered. So he slept in barns and ate with a traveller's dignity, seated by the roadside with his handkerchief spread on his knees and his feet dangling into ditches filled with gentians. He often thought of his wife in these moments. It was she who had first shown him that the world had flowers.

On the seventh day of his journey, walking longer through the twilight than had been his custom and looking in vain for a barn in which to sleep, he began to have the distinct sensation that the sun had gone down more than once. There were ponds and rifts filled with water in the fields, and the road was ribboned with long, wet reflections. Red. And orange. And yellow.

Flames.

At first, Symons imagined a forest fire, and he would have been content with this explanation if it hadn't been that a peasant driving a pregnant cow came toward him along the road and passed with a wave of his stick and a friendly greeting. Yet the sky was a violent array of colour, and the smell of smoke had thickened the air. Symons thought to himself, as he turned to watch the departing figure, that these were certainly extremely calm reactions to a forest fire – the waving of a stick, the gentle mutter of a cowbell, a smiling old man. Yet perhaps the old man was escaping, and the cow had been all that he could save. Symons' heart quickened.

As he rounded a bend in the road the scene before him made him wonder if he had come to a turning in his mind. He was thrown back violently into a setting that he had hoped was behind him forever.

In a field at the edge of a woods were two hundred men surrounded by fire: rows of flames with men and horses walking in between. Everyone was shouting, yet no one was running. Everything was burning, leaping in sheets of sparks through the air from great pits of heat, like a scene described in the kirk on Sundays: hell fire and brimstone. The Inferno. Yet no one seemed to be afraid. Not even the children he could see on the perimeters, nor the women who toiled with long, thick poles over what he could now make out to be pots so massive they were grotesque. It was as if a wash was being done in the fields of hell, and all the people had been reduced in size, or were hideous dwarfs.

Symons began to tremble. Cold sweat trickled down his sides. He was unarmed: he wanted a stick or a stone or a pitchfork with which to defend himself.

His immediate assumption was that someone must be forcing all this activity. It was so like the scenes he had left behind in Paisley: the women and the children and the harrowing concentration of their labour. He looked at the edges of the field, where he thought he would surely discover the gleam of bayonets and the sweating, scarlet tunics of a new-world militia. But there were no such sights to be found. There seemed to be, instead, an almost alarming camaraderie: laughter, endearments, friendly exhaustion as men sat down together and drank from the same pails of water; smiling, crooning women sat on chairs beneath the trees with their babes pressed against their breasts and the bairns asleep at their feet. There was even music. Songs. "Bonnie George Campbell."

He had found his own people. He had come to Glengarry.

He stayed with them only two days. Having discovered what they were doing, he tried to become a part of it. They were potash-makers, working for cash, which Symons could all too readily use.

But now he found, with something of a panic, that he could not wield an axe, and that he was equally inept in the handling of a saw. His hands, too long softened through their daily contact with sheeps' wool and lanolin, cracked open and blistered and bled. His skin seemed incapable of forming callouses. His fingers, trained to a fineness of touch and precision worthy of a pianist, locked themselves around the handles of his implements and became so painfully moulded they could not be undone without the aid of the foreman.

The foreman's name was Boyd. He was fond of John Symons; he admired the young man's courage. He was also quick to perceive that the spirited anger in Symons, the anger and frustration that had prompted him to leave his home and come to Canada, could just as well harm him. The lad kept flailing away at the trees like a madman. He would do himself, or someone else, an injury.

"You've such a quick temper, boy. It doesn't let you see what you're up against," he said. "You're ruining those hands of yours – and you're not doing me any favours in the meantime – hacking away at those logs. You're not out to slaughter pigs, with that axe."

"Give me some time," was Symons' protest. "It's only that I haven't got the feel of it yet."

"I can't do that," said Boyd, in the nicest way he could muster. "The work has got to get done. And proper done. And safe. It wouldn't do to have you lose a leg." He took the axe away from Symons.

"But I need this job so bad," said the latter, still trying to resist the foreman's efforts. "What am I to do without it?"

"Go and rest now. Eat," said Boyd. "You and me will settle up in the morning." He was already handing the axe to someone else.

Symons fumed. The foreman's dismissal, with all its promise of settling up and wages, placed him firmly back in the centre of the unemployed and, worse, of the unemployable. He rankled. He felt discarded and bitterly ostracized. He crossed the burning field and threw himself down beneath the trees beside a man called Hallet.

Hallet was old, maybe sixty-eight or seventy. He had been in the Canadas so long he could barely remember his home in Devon. Back then, he'd been a farmer. Then a soldier. Now, approaching death, he regretted his enlistment.

"What I should'a done," he said, "the moment I landed here in '87 was to cut my own trees down and not them trees for the army. That was the ticket then, lad, with all this land goin' free to them as claimed it."

"There's no such thing as *free*," said Symons. "I never known it in my whole life."

Hallet, being old, could look on Symons' petulance and smile. Which he did. "Whoa down, boy! There's no one so free in these modern times as a lad your years, sittin' here in this place, lookin' out at all that land."

Symons was busy binding a bleeding hand in his handkerchief. "All them *trees*, you mean! Look at this!" He held his swollen fingers under Hallet's nose. "I canna hold the axe!"

"You will, betimes. It comes after practice. Years. There's no born talent for it."

"Aye, but there is a born talent for starving."

"No one's starvin' here," said Hallet, indignant that Symons should even think so. "This is not what you've left behind, you know. It's not like home, where they bend you backwards till you break." He studied Symons' face. "*You* could take on the land. That's what the young, like you, are good for. Not a bad use for all that passion of yours. *And* you'd be your own master."

Symons looked at the old man's face.

Hallet concluded, "At least when you break your hands and your back it won't be to someone else's will, only to your own."

Symons trembled at the thought of it. Land. His own land. The last word in freedom. Still, the fact of his ignorance, the fact that he knew not a single thing about the land or the trees or the husbandry of beasts – this overwhelmed him. He dismissed it with a shrug. "Agh," he said, "I could never call myself a farmer."

Hallet was shrewd. He knew what Symons was all about. He knew that such complainers fail unless they are constantly challenged and pushed. He turned the screw. "Any man's a farmer," he said, "who's looking for independence."

Later, himself old and dying, Symons would recall that conversation in his own attempts to force his sons to seek independence of his wealth. Now it served as reconciliation with the fact of his own survival. Here he was, in a new land, having been tried by circumstance and found wanting. Hallet offered a remedy. Symons unwillingly, but wisely, accepted it. The remedy was wilderness. And will power.

❈

He followed roads and rumours. He had no access to real maps, although from time to time someone would draw him a route march in the dust.

He continued to use the river as his geographic mentor, supposing that, like a horse, it "knew the way." In a month he was in Prescott. There he was advised to journey on to Kingston in the hopes of finding a job.

Kingston was a fortified militia town. It was a seat of local government and a focal point for farmers from as far away as thirty miles. It had the makings of a city and held out promise to anyone with enterprise. Symons even heard of sheep farmers in the vicinity and thought he might find work in his own craft. For the first and only time in his travels he took a public conveyance, riding by coach from Prescott to Gananoque. Here, he was met with disaster.

There was an outbreak of typhoid fever. It was mild enough, but threw the fear of God into people; and Kingston closed its gates. Having just made a capital outlay in order to pay for the coach ride, Symons found himself most in need of work at the very moment when none was to be had. It was mid-July. He headed inland, west and north of the highway.

One evening he came to a broken-down farm. The fences were in desperate need of mending; the garden was untended with its vegetables overgrown with weeds and, in the yard, there was a dead cow.

Symons paused by the gate. A woman watched him from the door. She had a grey, unhealthy colour and a gaunt, exhausted expression. The woman held a spoon in her hand, as if she had been cooking when she heard him on the road.

"Good day."

The woman squinted and ran her fingers over her mouth, almost as if she were trying not to speak. Then, at last, she nodded at him.

"You," she said, "I never seen before."

"No, ma'am. I'm just passing through."

"You got some place to go in a hurry?"

"Only that I'm looking for somewhere to settle."

"Yes. And you're a Scot."

"Aye."

"My husband," said the woman and waved the spoon back into the room in which she stood. "My husband is from Perth."

"Aye."

"Maybe you will stay for supper."

"Yes, ma'am. I would like that."

She hooked her chin at him. He started up the lane. A cloud of flies rose from the dead cow. Symons passed to one side. The woman watched him carefully. She was gauging his honesty. And maybe more. He walked as straight as he could in spite of his hunger, and when he got to the door the woman was still standing in his path.

Their eyes met. He could see she was troubled.

"Come in," she said at last.

Symons sat at her table and wondered at the quiet in the house.

"You got no children," he said.

"No," said the woman. She stirred whatever was in the pot over the fire and set the spoon down on the hearth. Her back was to him. Without turning, she spoke again.

"Will you do something for me?" Her voice was barely audible.

"Aye. If I can."

"Go in there," she whispered and gestured at a room that stood darkened beyond a half-closed door. "Please," she added.

Symons rose and went towards the door. The atmosphere was heavy and hot. The woman still would not look his way. She was kneading her dress with her hands and her profile was outlined with sweat. He noticed now that her dress was utterly soaked with perspiration. He looked as best he could into the room beyond the door, but all he could see was the foot of a bed and an old, broken chair. The curtain was drawn across the window.

"Please," said the woman again. "Please. I cannot."

Symons approached the door almost on tiptoe and pushed it wide. For a second, he could not recognize the sound he heard, and then he realized. He'd already heard it in the yard: it was flies.

He walked in beyond the door and turned to his left where the sound had come from.

In the bed, there was a man lying with his back to Symons, apparently asleep.

The flies, only about a dozen, settled again around the man's right ear. Symons waited in itchy suspense for him to swat them away. But they remained. The man did not move; he did not even shiver. Symons involuntarily scratched his own ears, and it was then, still staring at the man, that he realized the meaning of the quiet.

"Sir?" he said and approached the bed.

The man did not stir. Symons looked back through the crack in the door to see if the woman had moved. She had not, except to turn her head in his direction, listening.

Symons reached out and touched the man on the shoulder, brushing away the flies.

Back in the other room with the woman, he did not need to speak.

"I was right, then?" she asked.

Symons nodded.

"I dared not know it," she said. "I simply couldn't bear to know it was true."

She picked up the spoon and stirred the contents of the pot.

"I been here all day, out here in this room. And all last night I slept in that chair" – she nodded at the corner – "knowing it was true. But I couldn't go in." She looked out the door at the yard. "He only came down with it four days back. The typhoid. Only four days ago. Then the cow died. And I –" She stopped. Then she sat down. Nothing more was said.

Symons told her he would bury both the man and the cow, and for this he would ask no wages other than his food. If she would let him fix her fences, he would do so for a modest fee.

The woman accepted. He buried the man that night and the cow the following morning. The woman did not weep until they both were underground.

Symons stayed with her three weeks, at which time her brother arrived from York with his wife. When Symons left them, he carried away a memory of kindness he would not forget and a sense of having achieved some good through his actions. But he also carried away the troubling memory of the nights he slept on the parlour floor with the woman only steps away in the dark. Until the keenness of her immediate presence had prompted him, he hadn't known there was so much carnality in his nature. He vowed he would never again allow himself that kind of proximity to women until his wife was by his side. He was young. He was intelligent. But he was not aware that he was civilized.

The evenings cooled. The nights brought frost, but the days remained as sunny and warm as any he remembered. Mists rose at morning. Sometimes he could see for miles from the heights he gained one by one. He swam through rivers, naked and exhilarated, holding his belongings over his head with one hand. In the evenings he built fires and became adept at telling the sounds of the forest. He lost his fear of bears. For a while. Until he saw one loping along through the trees one morning. After that he changed his stick for a stave and slept every night in the open or remained awake with fires. He travelled this way until September, stopping only when necessary for wages.

The place he came to in the end had the name of Simcoe's Corners. There it rained and he found himself in the middle of a muddy street near a cart that was so bogged down it had sunk to its axles. Out of sheer curiosity – there being no people by – he regarded the cart as if it were his duty to free it from the mud, and decided what was needed was a board.

It was not until after he made this inspection and came to this conclusion that he found he was himself being inspected from the sidewalk. Two dogs were watching, and a man, hunkered down with his back against the wall of a wooden store. This man wore a wide-brimmed hat of a kind that Symons had never seen, and he also wore a blanket around his shoulders like a cape.

"You the owner of this cart?" he said to the man.

"That's right."

"What you want is a board," said Symons.

"Yes," said the man in the rain hat. "But there is no board."

"But there must be a board," said Symons, eyeing, for instance, the boards of the wall against which the man was resting his back.

"I tell you, there is no board anywhere," said the man. Symons, looking up, perceived the very board they could use. There was lettering on it. OBADIAH CLARENCE BROWN. GENERAL MERCHANDISE AND LAND OFFICE. Symons pointed at it. The man with the hat stood up.

"We mustn't," he said.

"*You* mustn't," Symons said. "But I can, being a stranger." And he took down the board with a smile.

Within seconds, they were fitting it under the wheels of the cart and brawling in the mud like boys on a holiday. The dogs started barking, not only the two that had sat on the sidewalk against the wall, but five or six others, making their appearance from various doorways up and down the street.

Suddenly the air was clapped with the sound of a banging door. Looking up, Symons saw a tall, thin man in an apron.

"Watch it!" said the man in the hat. "There's Wellington."

Wellington was standing on the porch and shouting his head off in a high-pitched falsetto. "Hooligans! Riff raff! Thieves!"

Almost at once, whether because of the blood stains marking his butcher's apron or because of his reedy and alarming voice, Mr Wellington found himself surrounded by several yapping dogs, who threw themselves at his shoulders and face, dancing about on their hind legs.

"Scat! Scat! Be off!" Mr Wellington screamed, and disappeared inside the store.

"Now we're for it," said the man in the hat. "He's gone to get Mr Brown. Oh, what a mess I'm in! This cart is not my own, and now we'll have Obadiah down our backs!"

Symons was more concerned about the mud. "One more heave," he said, "and we've got it out."

They both got down behind the cart with its wheels on the board, and pushed so hard that they were flattened. But the cart had been moved; they had freed it. Symons swam in the mud, quite content to lie there, exhilarated and happy.

"What's your name, then?" he asked the man in the hat.

"Mathew Clark! You maniac!" screeched a voice from the sidewalk.

The man in the hat put his hand out and Symons took it, still lying full length.

"I'm Mathew Clark. The maniac," the man said. "How do you do?"

And that was how they met, in the mud of Simcoe's Corners: Mathew Clark and John Symons, who were to neighbour each other for thirty years.

Symons, of course, had to pay for the sign, but Obadiah Brown was somewhat mollified once he discovered the purpose of Symons' being there. Land.

"No," Brown kept repeating, as they perused the maps and charts of the district and its unclaimed lots. "You would not like it there." In guiding John Symons through the rigamarole of putting down his money and making his choice, he was both helpful and strangely insistent.

"There, there and there – all terrible. Terrible. But *here*." He tapped his finger on the word SURVEY printed over a small, drawn rectangle. "Here is exactly what you want. Mr Wellington, wouldn't you agree?"

Mr Wellington nodded sagaciously and tripped over his broom. "Most decidedly," he said, not even looking at the chart. "Oh, most decidedly indeed, Mr Brown."

It was not, however, on Mr Wellington's advice that Symons accepted Obadiah Brown's suggestion. It was because the lot he had been shown was next to Mathew Clark's. That alone decided him.

"This land," said Obadiah Brown, "is on the property of a man called Ellice. Mr Ellice requires, of course, a fee for the land he lets out."

"I have some money," said Symons.

"I'm *very* glad to hear it, sir. Hah-hah! A man of property!" And he poked at Symons with a finger.

His laughter was absolutely dead-eyed and mirthless. "Well, well, well, Mr Wellington!" he shouted. "Our community grows!"

"Yes, sir! Indeed it does!" said Mr Wellington, brushing at one of many cats with his broom. "Indeed, it grows by leaps and bounds."

"Well now! *Mister* Symons!" said Brown. "That'll be ten dollars down – and ten cents rent per acre per annum."

Symons fished through his belongings for his wallet.

Obadiah Brown bent over his papers, making marks and checks that Symons could not decipher. Brown continued speaking into the counter, almost inaudible. "There will be the road tax, of course. And you will grind your corn at Mr Ellice's mill. And for that privilege you will give one tenth of your meal to Mr – er, uhm – to *him*, but of course I mean to me, since I am his agent here and I act on his behalf in all things. Poor Mr Ellice, whose health demands that he reside outside the county. There now! Mr Wellington, if you would be so kind as to bring them down? A location ticket for Mr Symons! Thank you!"

Symons already knew enough about absentee landlords and grafting agents from his life in Paisley. For the moment, it only amused him to discover that, even in a new world, much was the same as in the old. But he could not let it affect him now. He was happy. He had found his home.

❈

Events were crowded by winter's approach.

Symons slept under canvas and every day he went out and walked his perimeters, looking again and again at his claimstakes, barely able to believe the extent of his boundaries. His land was covered with trees. On his second day of residence he began to cut them down. He still had no more talent with the axe than he'd possessed in the potash fields, but now that the trees and the clearing he wanted to make were his own, his hands did not become so desperately sore. What troubled him, in spite of his joy at having become a landed tenant, was the slowness with which

the clearing widened. He took down all the small trees first – the mountain ash, the poplar and the birch. This took him days: each tree had to be cut into lengths and piled for firewood. One day, he cut down twenty. And yet he hardly seemed to make a dent in the space he envisaged as being necessary if he were to put up the cabin he must have before the snow flew.

The nights grew longer. The hours he could not work increased, and became hours of torment. He was not only lonely for Margaret, he was lonely for company of any kind. The distance between the limits of his land and the Clarks' abode was something over a mile through the bush. Symons had never had any great affection for cat or dog, but now he wished he had a dog to hunt with, one that would sleep by his feet at night, and to which he could speak from time to time. His body ached for the warmth that only something alive can provide, and his hands itched for the feel of life in another creature.

He also discovered, to his dismay, that he had begun to mutter to himself as he worked. He even complained aloud of his own behaviour and mistakes. "Don't do that, you loony!" he would say when something was spilled or broken. "See! You done it wrong!" he would shout when he felled a tree on top of another. "Look where you're going!" he said when he tripped. He began to bite his lips to prevent these inadvertent speeches. He became unnervingly aware that he was in danger of madness or what to him would pass for madness – anything betraying weakness. For if the weakness were to dominate his reason, he would be lost.

❈

One morning when he woke, the stillness and the quiet were almost oppressive. Something was wrong, but he could not decipher what it was. He lay in his tent, wrapped in every bit of wool and cloth and fur that he possessed. His body was too stiff with fatigue to rise, and his brain seemed paralysed. And yet he knew he must discover what was wrong. There was not even bird song.

Symons forced himself to push his legs out

straight away from the centre of his own warmth. He uncurled his fingers and made them massage his arms so the blood would flow.

At last, when he'd crawled from his blanket roll and put on his boots, he looked out, expected to see the world he had gone to sleep in, but saw, instead, a world of brilliant white. All through the night it had snowed. And now the sun was shining.

Not far off – too close for comfort, he thought – a fox or a wolf was barking in the woods. Symons spun to the sound of it, reaching for his axe. He fell down. His legs were still asleep.

Another wolf or fox began to bark. Symons pulled himself to the axe and grasped it by the handle, still lying in the snow.

What was happening?

A man stepped out of the trees. He, too, was carrying an axe.

All at once, he was surrounded. By giants. Or so it seemed. And they all carried axes.

He was barely able to find his voice, but at last he managed to stand and speak.

"What do you want?" he asked.

"You be John Symons?" This from the giant nearest to him.

"Aye. And what of it?" He was holding the axe defensively in front of his chest.

"We come here to cut down your trees," said the giant. "And put up your cabin." Then he extended his hand. His name, he said, was Dowson, and no sooner had he told it than he gave a great wild shout to the woods. "Clear land!" And twenty axes started felling the trees.

Symons could hardly protest. He was dazed.

When Mathew Clark came up to him, he said, "Who are these fellows, Matt? What does it mean?"

Clark explained it was the local custom. Something called a "bee." One day, Symons would be called upon to help clear someone else's land. In the meantime, he could start to organize his cabin.

Some of the men had brought oxen and horses. As the trees were felled and the giant bonfires lit

from the brush, the logs were dragged to the cabin site where men, whose trade it seemed to be, set about notching them and putting them in place. The chinks between the logs were stuffed with moss. Space for a round tin chimney was cut in one wall. Symons must eventually purchase (on credit, of course) a stove from Obadiah Brown. They thought of everything. They even built him a bunk and a table, and shelves. Throughout it all, Symons stood with his mouth half open, incredulous and even suspicious. He could not believe it was happening. Or the speed with which they worked. By the day's end they had it all done, and Symons was standing with Clark and his dog in the newly made clearing, before his own front door.

"I have brought you this," said Clark drawing a package from his knapsack.

"What?" said Symons, beaming. He had not received a gift for years.

"Open it," said Clark. "It's my Emily that's done it."

Symons drew aside the burlap wrappings and found he was holding a shiny glass funnel and a pewter dish.

"It's a lamp for your candles," said Clark.

And then he was gone.

That night, long after dark, Symons sat in his coat and his gloves at his new table. He was seated on a stump, dragged in from the heap outside. The lamp had been lit twenty minutes now, and had not guttered once. Symons stared and stared at its shining light. He felt transported through the reflections of the glass to the fireside of his mother's cot in Paisley. There sat his wife and his mother and his sisters.

Yet, all around him there was silence, thousands of miles of trees and snow and wilderness and ocean.

He blew out the candle. He was emphatically alone.

Late in February the wind blew unceasingly for three days. Snow fell for two of these days, and when, at last, he was able to emerge from his hut it was only after digging up through a tunnel. There was a drift so deep it hid his roof.

The insulation of the drift made his cabin warm. But the warmth would diminish at night. He had bring in stacks of fuel for the stove, in case he got completely snowed in. The trouble was that, because of the drifts, he could not find his woodpile. He would have to seek fresh supplies of firewood from the forest.

So he struck out, carrying his axe, and soon found a grove of dead birch. He chose a tree and began to cut it down. He was standing too far away; the axe glanced off the bark and buried itself in the snow. Symons retrieved it and, taking a firmer stance, swung again.

He was hardly aware of how it happened. The axe glanced off the tree and came towards him just as he felt himself sinking through the surface of the drift on which he stood. His initial sensation was one of frustration. He was angry. Thwarted. Trees, he thought. The bastards! He reached down through the snow, meaning to bring up the axe, which had buried itself out of sight with the force of his swing. What he brought up instead was a handful of flesh.

His first unthinking reaction was to put it back. He drew his leg up out of the snow. And fainted. The leg was nearly severed. The flesh had been cut away from just above the knee.

When he woke he began to cry for help, afraid that he would bleed to death. Of course, there was no response. The Clarks were over a mile away and there was no one else.

He bound up his leg with his scarf.

At first he tried to hobble, but the pain was terrible. He fell so many times that at last he began to crawl.

His journey took him hours. For most of it, he made his way between the trees by "swimming" through the snow. Time to time he fainted dead away and would awaken thinking hours had passed. In fact, he lost consciousness for no more than minutes. Still, the journey took its toll. When darkness began to close around him he was lost.

After nightfall he collapsed for what he thought must be the last time. He was reconciled to dying. If he did not bleed to death, then surely he must freeze.

A wolf began to bark.

Symons gave a primal shout of rage. He would be eaten. They would find his bones. It maddened him. Margaret faded in and out of his mind.

He rose and stood beneath the trees. He would fight the wolf with his bare hands.

He could see it, looming grey against the moonlit snow. It was huge. It bristled. Growled. And leapt.

Symons caught it by the throat. Its teeth were snapping at his face.

And then its snarling faded and seemed to caress him. It began to lick his cheeks and to whimper some kind of welcome.

Symons fell back.

It was Mathew Clark's dog.

Emily Clark had a habit of surviving catastrophe. As a child, she had been the lone survivor of a shipwreck in which her parents had died. Finding herself, at twelve, the oldest of six orphaned children, she made it her business to see they would survive. She became their mother, father, aunts, uncles, spiritual guide, and teacher. She got them all through accidents, desperate poverty, and diseases, and, in the meantime, she got herself an education. In the winter of 1828, she put her experience to use, and not only saved John Symons' life, but improved his lot as well.

Her first accomplishment was to save his leg. This she did by sewing it back together and by an endless application of poultices and dressings made of herbs and medicinal powders. She urged his circulation to survive the shock by judicious and expert massage. And she kept his spirit alive by her patience and her humour.

All the while, Mathew Clark proudly watched his friend revive and helped his wife as a nurse might help a doctor. The Clark children, too, kept the cabin bright with their games and their constant fascination with things found in the bush and brought back home to show off. By the time spring arrived, the window sills and mantle were crowded with bits of fantastic wood and stones, birds' nests, bones and dried leaves and grasses.

In time, Symons was able to sit up, though he rested his leg full length on the bed Matt had made for him by the fire. He was not allowed to walk.

One afternoon, while Mathew was making a crutch and the children were helping their mother dip candles and twist wicks, Emily said, "Why don't you entertain us, John?" And she handed him a book from which to read aloud.

"I would," Symons said. "But I can't."

"You need more light?" Mathew asked.

"No. I mean . . ."

Emily was watching him.

"I can't read," Symons said. He felt ashamed, for he knew that even the children could read.

"Never mind," said Emily. "You can tell us a story."

Symons told them the story of his father's death and the Paisley riots and his own escape.

"It is like my shipwreck," Emily said.

"Yes," said Symons. "And this country is the island to which we have swum."

Everyone laughed. And then Emily said, "I like that, about this being an island. It's just like Robinson Crusoe."

"Who is he?" said Symons, never having heard of him.

"The man in that story," said Emily, pointing at the book she had given him. "In fact, I think there can be no better way for you to begin your learning than with that."

In two weeks time, Symons was entertaining the Clarks with the tale of Robinson Crusoe. "*I was born in the year 1632, in the city of York, of a good family,*" he read.

Emily also taught him how to write. Day by day he mastered the letters of his first word.

M A R G A R E T.

As May was beginning Symons was hopping around the Clarks' cabin using a crutch, and on occasion setting the toes of his damaged leg on the boards. He was able now to sit at the table, and it was there, one night by lamplight, that he wrote his first letter.

"*Margaret. Come. There is a house and I am well. Be quick.*"

This was the message he had always wanted to send, but now he added something new, on impulse: "*Bring books.*" To which he appended his whole name: *John Alexander Symons.*

Emily looked at what he had written. "But she won't know which books to bring."

"Does it matter?" Symons asked.

Emily smiled. "No," she said. "I guess it doesn't. I guess it doesn't matter at all."

The Irish

Ireland, once the intellectual centre of Europe, was severely weakened by a century of raids from the Northmen of Scandinavia, and left vulnerable to a more powerful enemy –the Normans. A century after they occupied England, the Normans conquered Ireland, ultimately bringing it under the British crown.

By the 1690's, Ireland's population was one-third Catholic. For over one hundred years after King James II was defeated by Protestant William of Orange, the Irish were politically suppressed, their land was given to Protestants, and they were the victims of severe religious persecution. In 1801, the Act of Union officially joined Ireland and Great Britain both politically and economically, but Catholics were deprived of the vote until 1829 and, under the law, could not be educated.

In 1845 the first reports of "potato disease" occurred and the government of Robert Peel began emergency relief programs. The potato was the staple, and often the only food of the Irish peasant and Peel's government was not insensitive to the results of the potato blight. Unfortunately, Peel's attempts to repeal the Corn Laws in order to import corn for the Irish caused a landlord revolt and the defeat of his government. The potato crop failed again in 1846 and unprecedented famine struck. It was most severe in seven districts, where the potato was the only crop, and it was here that the cottiers, tenants with less than an acre of land, suffered the most.

Weakened by hunger and cholera, the Irish fell easy prey to typhus, which had long been endemic in the land. By 1847, the entire Irish economy had been affected: the peasants were starving, disease swept the industrial centres, and merchants went into bankruptcy. Those who had money booked decent passage for North America; the poor were packed into ancient ships by their landlords and sent off penniless to face the unknown. The sick mingled with the healthy, and disease broke out on nearly every vessel.

By December 1847 the Canadian authorities had inspected over 1,400 ships for typhus, and when the disease broke out in Canada the newly arrived immigrants were blamed. Even the healthiest and hardest working of the Irish were often forced to accept humiliating working conditions in order to begin to prosper, and thereby to counter the vicious prejudice they faced in their early years in Canada.

1847

One hundred thousand men, women, and children fled the famine and disease of Ireland. They were leaving a poverty-stricken and starving land for another world. There, if the streets were not exactly paved with gold, surely they would find a better living – work, food, land – than the one they knew. Filled with hope they set out on a grim journey. Many would never reach the new land, but the letters and journals of the few who could read and write tell us of their voyage.

*"Each emigrant was allowed by law
thirty-three inches of room in width"*

"On each side of the vessel, 'between decks,' were two
rows of bunks, one above the other. These were made of
boards; each bunk held two persons, and the division
between bunks was nothing but a narrow strip of lumber. They might properly be described as an upper and a
lower bunk running all round the ship. The hold was
simply a large floating cellar."

"A cloud of melancholy hung over us"

"In those days, everybody in the Old Country thought that if they only had their passage paid to America, their fortune was made.... [There the] pineapples, rich and mellow, grew in profusion, grapes hanging in enormous bunches from the vines over-shadowing the rivers so that the men as they paddled their canoes had but to stretch out their hands and pluck the rich clusters. Game of all kinds in the greatest abundance – all a man wanted was a gun and ammunition to be able to live like a Prince."

For many the hope of life was to end in death

"We were just two weeks out when the first of our number died. It was a calm, hot night. There was not a breath of air. I saw him die. He had been sick in his bunk but a few hours, and had risen to get a drink of water; he was on his way back, but sat on his trunk to rest himself. Shortly after he lay back and died. I can see him now."

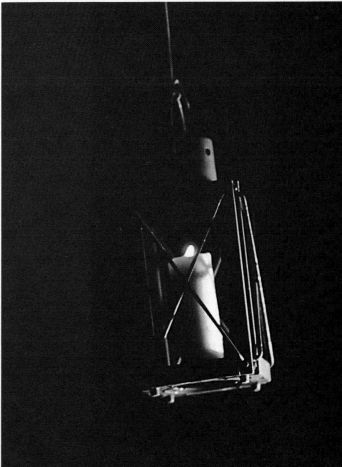

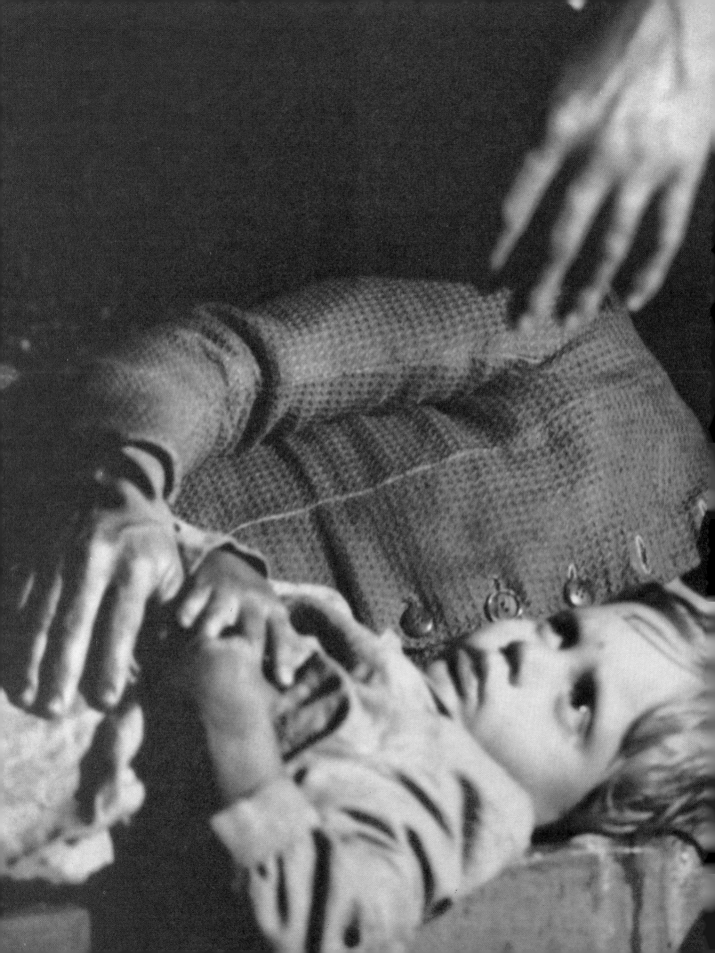

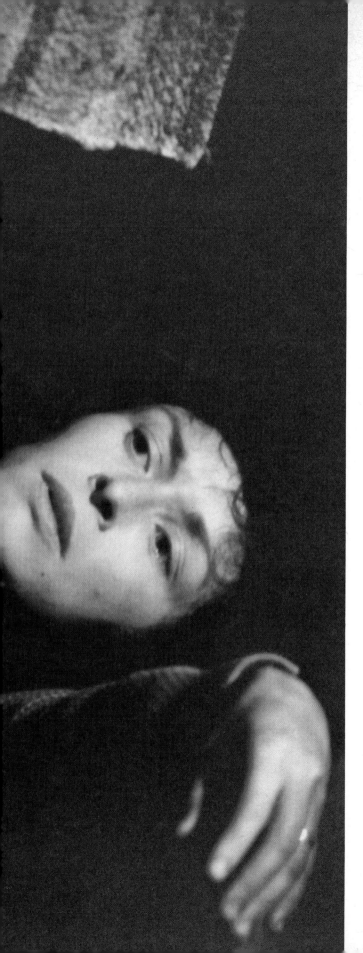

"From this time forth the deaths were frequent and sudden. Sometimes we would go a couple of days without any deaths at all, and sometimes we would bury two or three a day. One day, six people died, and we threw them overboard. Those whose friends had money got a better funeral than the others. They were sewed up in cloth by the sailors, and they had weights to sink them. Those who could not afford this were thrown overboard exactly as they died."

Starvation, neglect, despair, typhus and
death travelled with them. Some 17,000
Irish perished during the voyage, a further
20,000 on shore. A witness wrote: "If crosses
and tombs could be erected on the water,
the whole route of the emigrant vessels
would long since have assumed the
appearance of a cemetery."

A Better Place Than Home

ALICE MUNRO

Mary looked down from the window above her father's shop and saw a pig that some country people were driving to market. It was so gaunt you could hardly tell it was meant to be a pig, but the family behind it must have starved themselves to keep it alive, hoping to sell it. This was Fair Day, and there would be more sights like that, more raggedy, pitiful, beggarly people. Every such sight Mary kept to tell her father at tea time, and when they lit the fire and drew the curtains and sat down – she and her father, who was a widower, and her youngest sister, and her own little boy, James, who was just out of dresses – she would say, "Oh, Father, isn't it desperate the state the country is in?"

And she and her father and even her sister would know that it wasn't the state of the country she was talking about at all. What she was saying was, if things are so bad, then James is not to blame. She had some idea that if things got bad enough, and all the stories of ruin and starvation were true, nobody would be blamed anymore or go to prison for their debts – which is what would have happened to James if her father had not got him on the boat to Quebec – and some great rescue would occur. Long afterwards, she thought that such an idea simply showed how comfortably she had been brought up, and how ignorant she was of life.

"Bad enough," her father might say, but his own shop had not suffered much. Ladies who bought wool and linen and silk were still buying. He did not depend, as James had done, on the custom of poor people. And Mary knew, too, that if her father were to go out collecting what was owing him, he would not come back and say, as James had said, that the family was barefoot and had no chairs but had rolled up a stone for him to sit on, and how could you ask for money from people like that. No, her father would have looked around and seen whatever they had, one good cloak maybe, or a kettle, and taken that, till he was paid.

The baby began to whimper in the cradle. Mary's sister, Sadie, ran into the room and started the cradle rocking. She was one of those young, unmarried girls who were besotted over babies. Let her be. Mary loved her children well enough, but her thoughts were full of James. No one else mentioned him. They behaved as if his boat had dropped off the edge of the world, and Mary and her young James and the baby, Annie, were settled here for good, back home, safe and content, keeping Sadie and the old man company. Mary did not see that as her future. She meant to go to James within a year, and she planned a steady campaign of harassment, stubbornness, and cajolery, such as she had waged four years before when she made up her mind to marry him although he was poorer, better looking, and freer in his manners than anybody her father would have chosen.

The boat was one used to bring lumber back from Quebec. Instead of ballast, it took out Irish emigrants. The bunk was hardly wide enough for James' narrow haunches, and he wondered how a stout person would manage. But he saw no stout people aboard. There were a few, like himself, who looked decently fed, who had overcoats and boots and travelling bags; but most were thin and poor, and came with their cooking pots, their spoons and scissors – whatever they possessed – hanging from belts or a rope around their waists, and you could not tell if the wrappings they wore were cloaks or blankets. Next to him was a family of this description, a weak-looking man who was a cooper by trade, his young, worn wife, a newborn baby, a girl about the age of young James, and a boy a couple of years older. In the bunk above was a fellow worse off than those; he had only one garment on him, either a long shirt or a short coat, and carried nothing but a shillelagh. He was at least six feet tall and thin as a stick, with long knobby bare legs stretching far over the end of the bunk. He had a wild look. Likely he came from the west country, from Donegal or Mayo. James had heard desperate stories about those places, about villages where every soul had died, about corpses bloated in the ditches and starving children, whose tongues clove to the roof of their mouths so they could not speak. It was said that the people there had lost all the hair on their heads in the last stages of starvation, but hair had grown on their faces and bodies, pale corpse hair that grew from them so they looked like dogs. It was not only starvation there; they had the fever. Look out this fellow had not brought it with him.

The man stuck his head over the edge of the bunk and spoke upside down.

"Ye're not from County Mayo, are ye?"

Sure enough.

"No," said James, and tried to stare into space.

There was no space. Everywhere he looked he saw a human face, not one of them happy, until he noticed the little son of the family next to him. The boy's legs were braced to feel the ship's motion under him, his eyes were amazed and approving.

"Ye're from the south?"

"No," said James. "From County Louth."

"I never thought there was so many Irish in the world. They're from every part of it. But nobody from Mayo I can find to talk to." He hung his head lower and said in a sharp whisper, "Did ye know they let the Orangemen on?"

James did not answer.

"Ye're not an Orangeman yourself?"

"No."

The woman next to James was listening. She was doing more. She was fixing up a rag curtain to separate herself and her family from James and the man above.

"Did ye leave yer family behind then?" said the man more gently, and James thought he must be showing his feelings plain on his face for this fellow or anybody to see, and indeed how could he help it? Every time the boat rose and fell on the water he thought of the separation. Six weeks at sea, they said. Six weeks crowded like pigs in a pen with this unlucky lot, and then a country he could not imagine; forests and wolves and snow. But they had shops there, as at home. He had a letter in his pocket to Mr Thomas Sheridan, who had a shop at a place called Brantford, in Canada West. As soon as he could get settled, working for this Mr Sheridan, he would send for Mary and pray God her father would send her cabin class, never on a boat like this one. Within a year he might see her again.

"I left my wife," he said. "And my two children."

"Well. It's a curse on a man to have a family. I was spared it myself. I couldn't marry while my mother was alive and no sooner was she gone than the landlord, he doubled the rents. So I waited. I waited so long, I lost the inclination."

The first storm started at night. The fellow above swung his legs down and hit James in the chest and yelled with all his strength, "Mercy on us, the ship's going down!"

There was howling and confusion. The lanterns were blown out. Most people struggled to the ladders and climbed on deck, as if they would rather be washed over than die in the dark. Every wave opened for them like a dragon's mouth. They plunged in, were half-drowned, then miraculously rode free. Some people were retching so hard they could not stop to pray; others called over and over on the saints and the Virgin. The man from Mayo was in a rapture of fear, casting himself on the deck and crying to Saint Patrick, Saint Christopher, Saint Michael, and the Mother of God. The Protestant family did not weep or pray or vomit, but crouched together and held themselves tight in their Protestant way. James had been sick the day before in a mild swell, but he was not sick now. He was terrified and elated.

A sailor yelled at him that if he was not needed for the praying he could come below to the pumps, and he did so. It was a long time since he had known so simple a thing to put his strength to. There was another passenger working with him, a big rosy country boy, one of the few on board who looked as if he had not gone hungry lately. James was flat out trying to match him, but he did, and even spent some breath on conversation.

"What d'you think we'll see first, will it be Quebec or the bottom of the sea?"

The sailors laughed. "Oh you won't be drowned in this. Ye'll see a half-dozen more like it before we get to the other side."

When they came on board all their food parcels had been taken from them, to be returned, the sailors said, as soon as the ship sailed. Ten days later James sat on the deck with the others, listening to the names called and thinking of the cooked ham Mary had packed for him. Those who had got their parcels removed themselves as much as possible, seeking privacy as animals do for the first tasting of their food. At a distance, but watching, were those who had brought no food. They had to live on the ship's ration of biscuit and barley meal. Some of them said they had seen big loaves of bread in the shipping agent's window, and were convinced they would get bread aboard. Of course they got no such thing.

"Mary Dillon! John O'Reilly! George Rorsdan! James Thompson!"

James took the package to the rail and tore at the wrappings. He had thought he was hungry plenty of times in his life, but he had never worshipped meat like this. Even if he had Mary here, would he spare her a bite? He would, he would; but nobody else that he could think of.

He was raising it to his mouth when he saw it was full of maggots. Not an inch free, they popped from the rosy meat like sweat. The whole ham was writhing with them. His stomach heaved. He threw the ham into the water, and held on to the ship's rail, not knowing what to do, curse or bellow or weep. All would be useless. He took from his pocket the ship's biscuit, hard as wood. He sucked, and gnawed and gagged and swallowed, and got a rich smell of cheese. It was his friend from the pumps who stood cradling a big orange-gold cheese, stuffing chunks in his mouth. James could not stand the smell. He went and sat along the deck with his head between his knees.

Soon he noticed another smell, of fat pork. It grew stronger; he saw a woman's bare feet and crooked hem. It was his neighbour. Quick as could be she took her hand from under her shawl and lowered a tin cup to him. There was barley soup in it, bits of pork floating on the surface leaving a golden grease. Perhaps she didn't want her family to see her giving what was theirs. James took the cup, and gulped the soup. He was nearly weeping then in his hunger and humiliation, as he hadn't wept when he left Mary or when he put up the shutters on his shop.

That night James woke and saw the boy who had eaten the cheese groaning and tossing. His face was not rosy now but yellowish pale and glistening with sweat. Serve him right if he had stuffed himself to death.

Next day the fellow stayed below, and by night it was clear his trouble was more than overeating. Spots were coming out on him; he was raving with fever. His spots were red at first and small, then spread and turned brown, and a bad stench came from him. Nobody would go near. In the morning that strong, lively fellow was dead. It took three sailors to rope him up in canvas and drag him on deck.

The captain came and spoke over him. "Oh-Lord-we-commend-this-man-to-thy-keeping...." The rest of his words were lost.

The sailors tipped up the board he was on, and the body slid off, hit the water upright. It bobbed in the clear waves, and spun, and turned more slowly, and sank, still dimly visible, still playfully turning and bowing, on its way down.

No one would touch the cheese that had been under his head. The rats came and tore it, and squealed for joy.

"Is he at the bottom of the sea yet?" said the little boy, the Protestant boy whose name was William.

"Who is that?" said James, who had become friends with this family.

"The dead fella. That had the spots on him."

James said he did not know.

"Would the fish eat him?"

To take his mind off it, James started to make a cat's cradle of the string he had saved from that ham.

"Wouldn't it be a fine thing if we saw a fish now, and it was a big fat salmon, and we caught it, and cooked it for our dinner?"

Soon people were lying helpless in their sickness above and below deck. Some came out in fever spots, others lost all liquid from their bodies in watery white vomit and stools. After this they might live on and slowly recover if they were brought food and water, which they were too weak to get themselves. Or they might go blue around the eyes and mouth, and stiffen, and die. James and any other men in health were kept busy roping up and removing the dead. There was soon no canvas left, and the dead went in their rags, showing their own stiff faces to the ocean water. Anything good they had, a shirt or belt, was taken from them first. There was not so much squeamishness now; a bit of salt meat, a pouch of barley, maybe a turnip, and in one case a spicy blood-pudding were divided and enjoyed.

The father of the Protestant family took the cramps and the vomiting. He grew weak, his eyes sank in his head; but he lingered on and his wife was hopeful. One evening she asked James to hold the baby and mind the other children while she went to cook the soup. The ship was rolling. The man asked for water, and William tried to give him some from a cup, but he retched it up. The rolling got worse and the lanterns went out. Barrels and boxes and pots were rolling between the bunks, and helpless bodies, too. The children climbed on top of their father to be out of the way. By accident the boy touched his father's face, and screamed. His scream was lost in the noise of the storm. It was all James could do, for some time, to hang on to the baby. When he could, he reached over to the neighbouring bunk. His hand fell on the man's cold mouth still wet with the water he had tried to swallow.

After this storm, sailors came with ropes and lashed pails and barrels in place again. Some drinking-water was gone, and many private provisions. James saw a woman who had yesterday watched dry-eyed when her husband was tipped into the water. She was wailing because her tea canister had been washed away, and she had found it empty. Bedding was soaked, some people were cut and bruised, and there were more dead to be collected. The children's mother took down the rag curtain and wrapped her husband's face and neck in it, tying it securely, so she would not see his dead face going through the water. Then she took back her baby, laid her hand over the fluttering pulse at the top of its head, and sang to it, the same song she always sang.

The man from Mayo came on deck, and motioned James to a private corner. He had found a whisky bottle. There was not much in it.

"It wasn't me drank it, I swear to God. There was only that when I found it."

James believed him, and thought it rare generosity in anyone, to save that little to share.

When they entered the Gulf of St Lawrence the weather was fair, the water like silk; they could see the high shore with its crown and cover of trees, gulls dipping and crying. Not a house or barn or church to be seen, but the air was pleasant. People lay on deck and lifted their faces to the sun and the sweet air, but a smell of death and pestilence rose like a cloud from below.

The children's mother sat apart and rocked her baby. She had not made anything to eat that day. James took her barley-bag and made some soup for the children, and brought her some in a mug. She reached to take it, the shawl she had wrapped around herself and the baby fell away, so that James could see the little grey face, grey as a mouse, and the scalp where the pulse was not beating any more.

The woman hissed at him like a snake, and he thought she might be feverish, half-mad. But then her ordinary face returned, her young hollowed woman's face, and she whispered, "She died in the night. You won't tell nobody?"

He shook his head.

"You won't tell nobody? I don't want them to put her in the water. I want to bury her on the land. I want to bury her on the land."

She was not mad at all. Anybody could see you should not put a baby in the water. James held the cup and she drank a little, this time holding her shawl tight.

"Quebec is a grand-looking place," the man from Mayo was telling the children. "There's a fine-looking people there, and they put meat in with the potatoes three times a day."

"It's such a wholesome place the fever leaves you," he said. "It leaves you, once you set foot on the shore!"

The ship dropped anchor far out in the river. There was an island which seemed to float on the water, perfectly reflected, with its softly rising green shores, its low white buildings, what might be a church spire. Here at last was a place that looked like home. Boats were coming out to them from that island. All empty, except for the sailors rowing them. No, there was one boat with three or four men in it. One in a priest's hat.

The sailors were rounding up everybody who could stand. They said a doctor was coming, to look at their tongues. If your tongue was clean, you could go on and land at Quebec. If it showed a furry coat, you must get off here, and go to the hospital sheds on the island. The place was called Grosse Isle.

The priest went to the sick people, whom the sailors were roping up as they had roped the dead bodies, so that they could be lowered over the side and taken away in the boats. The doctor and his assistant stood by the rail, and the passengers passed in front of him one by one. It took him only a second to look and say, "Clean," or "Fur." Sometimes he only made a motion of his head. What if he got mixed up sometimes, or moved his head the wrong way? He looked too tired to care. The sailors took the people whose tongues were not clean to a place farther along the rail and prodded them over, on to the ladder. They kept close guard so that these people could not get loose and join the others whose tongues were clean and who would be allowed to land.

James stood in line with the two children and their mother. She had her pots and bundles tied around her. One of the bundles was the baby. Luckily her children had not noticed that her arms were empty; they were too interested in the proceedings, and alarmed by the appearance of the priest and the doctor.

"Put out your tongue," the doctor had to tell her twice, and when she did he made a movement of his head, that she should go to the rail. She seemed not to understand.

"Move on," the assistant said to her, and her hand tightened on the swaying bundle. She remembered her living children then, and turned to where James was letting them balance on his boots, to distract them. James turned them to face the doctor.

"Are those yours?" said the doctor, and the woman nodded.

"Take them with you then. Take them to the sheds."

The sailors pushed the children after her.

James moved up and opened his mouth.

"Clean," the doctor said. James' heart was pounding in his throat, his eyes filled with tears of relief. He went to join the people who needed no sailors to guard them. He looked for the mother and her children, but there were sailors and other people in the way. He heard the doctor say, "Clean. Clean. Fur." There was a cry of outrage.

"You're not seein' right, doctor! It's the wormy biscuit they give us! I'm as well as you and better. It's biscuit on my tongue!"

It was the man from Mayo. He looked ready to bolt, and he had his shillelagh. Three sailors moved in on him and pushed him, still howling protest, on to the ladder. There was such confusion around there that James did not see when the children and their mother went over the rail. Then he heard his name called from below. It was the boy calling him. He was calling clearly, through all the commotion, from the open boat.

"*James!*"

The Protestant boy, five years old, for whom he had made a cat's cradle, to whom he had told stories. He had protected him all he could and could not protect him any more.

He did not go to the rail to wave. What would be more useless and more cruel than that wave? The boy called two or three times more, then stopped. James could not bear to watch the boats pulling towards the island. He walked around the deck and looked at the dark luxuriant shore of this wild country.

He thought that he would never be able to tell anybody on shore what it had been like on the ship. They could not imagine. They were ignorant beyond belief; they were fortunate; they were fools.

When Mary got the letter she skipped all the parts about sickness and storms, because she did not want to be afraid of the voyage. Nor did she mention anything about that to her father.

"He's in Quebec," she said. "Oh, no, by now he'll be in Brantford. He'll probably be working already, and writing me to come over."

"We'll see how he does there," said her father.

"Thomas has done well there," said Mary. "You never stopped Elsie from going."

Elsie was her older sister. Thomas was Elsie's husband.

"Ah, Thomas," said her father. "He's a man that took up land."

"There's more to do there than be a farmer," said Mary, as if she knew all about it.

James had thought that only getting to Brantford would be a problem, not the beginning of more problems, and it was bad enough. Toronto was a wild rough town, with taverns everywhere and whores in their finery and carriages, with gangs of boys chasing them for pennies, and the dust flying, and signs in the windows of the workplaces.

NO IRISH NEED APPLY
NO IRISH OR DOGS

When they heard his voice, some laughed at him and told him to stay till Saturday and he'd see the hanging; they were hanging some Irishman for bashing another Irishman's head in. He did not know if it was a joke. But a man ran after him, out of the tavern, and told him decently enough that if he wanted to get to Brantford he must take the steamer, the *Passport*, to Hamilton, and then take the stage. Or he could go down to Coffin Block and take Boyce's Telegraph Stage, that would get him to Hamilton, too, but it was a rough ride.

"I'm much obliged," said James.

"You a Mick or an Orangeman?"

"I'm a Roman Catholic."

"It's a fact, isn't it, the one kind of Irishman can't abide the other kind, and they're all just Irish to us. Micks and Orangemen, breakin' each other's heads, and they're all just Irish to us!"

It was dark when they got to Brantford, with only some dim light from the windows and lanterns swinging from the tailgate of wagons. The black streets were full of potholes, and it was mostly by accident he found the right premises. But he could not doubt it, there was the sign: THOMAS SHERIDAN, GENERAL MERCHANT, HORSE DEALER.

Two men were just leaving the store. One would be Mr Sheridan.

But when James asked they looked at each other queerly, and said they were not.

"I wonder could you tell me where to find him?"

James was too eager to have his future settled to go back to the inn, and besides he had run short of money.

Again he thought he saw a queer look, but they began to direct him.

The house, if this was the right one, seemed to be full of lights and people. The door was open on the warm night, and people went in and out. James entered and saw a group of men standing around a whisky barrel, smoking pipes, drinking from a dipper, chewing tobacco. The smell of tobacco and horses and food cooking was thick and welcoming, and the voices were Irish. James took the letter from his pocket and spoke to a pair of girls who were giggling at him.

"I have a letter here for a Mr Thomas Sheridan."

The girls giggled louder. Girls were brash here. But a man nearby looked stern and said, "I'm thinking he'll not be caring to read it now, mister." He nodded towards another part of the room and at the same moment three women in black set up a wailing. They were keeners. There was a middle-aged, dignified-looking man lying in a coffin.

"Mr Sheridan?" said James.

"Himself."

Someone handed James the dipper. "Take a drink, mister. It'll do you good."

They were noticing the travelling bag and the dust on him.

"Have you come a long journey?"

"From Quebec," said James, "and from Belfast before that."

Then they were all around wanting to know about Ireland, and was there starvation where he came from? Was there fever? Was there sickness on the boat?

"There was some," said James. "But it could have been of the bad food." He knew enough not to spoil his welcome.

"But it's bad in the old country, isn't it? They say they lay down there and die in their own doorway. And nobody comes to bury them."

"It's bad," James said. "It's bad there." It seemed years to him since he had left home.

Meanwhile there were voices rising; and from what James could gather, the dead man had not died of any sickness, but of a kick from a horse. The relatives were saying somebody had sold him the horse without letting on the bad ways it had, and the man who had sold it – he had just come in – was saying that he was no liar and perhaps the animal had been mistreated. Then the relatives and those on their side were on to him and his side for speaking ill of the dead, and there was a blow struck; the fight began. There was too much noise for the keeners. They stopped their wailing and went to the whisky barrel to help themselves. The fighting spilled out into the yard. James helped himself to whisky. It was the same as a big country funeral at home.

The women came carrying platters of food to the table, and shouting to the men that they were fools if they would rather fight than eat. Some men came in with bloodied heads, and the women flipped up their dresses in a business-like way and tore off petticoat strips for bandages. James had eyes for nothing but the food. There was roast pork and fowl, roast apples, hot cakes, maple syrup, baked potatoes, muffins, giant loaves of pure white bread, dressed pigeons, preserves. He was afraid his greed would mark him out, but everyone there was just as greedy. Plates were heaped again and again, and mugs filled with tea and whisky. The only person who had time for anything else was the fiddler tuning up in the corner.

The fiddler played for a while without much notice being taken, but when interest in the food had waned some of the men began pushing the furniture aside, clearing the floor for dancing. The coffin was in the way, and they dragged it to one side and set it up on its end, so the corpse could stand and look on at the proceedings. Some women acted scandalized, but others shushed them and said hadn't he a right to look on, wasn't it his own wake?

From then on there was dancing and drinking, and more eating, more drinking, people falling asleep on the edges of the dance floor. James was drunker than he had been since his marriage. He danced with the girls who had giggled at him. They showed their petticoats and asked why he hadn't wanted a bandage. There was much freedom here and bold talk, but not much acting on the talk, as far as he could see. Perhaps it was the condition they were all in soon – and he as well — that saved them.

He woke with the soft, bare leg of a sleeping woman resting on his boot. It was just light. Sleepers and groaners were everywhere, the coffin back in place, and the keeners dozing over it, crusty faced. He got himself loose and stumbled towards the fresh air. He found it necessary to carry his head carefully, like a big boiled pudding on a plate.

"James says that drink is the great curse of the country over there, it is even worse than here, and he is going to find a temperance priest so he can take the pledge."

"Does he find it a temptation, then?"

Mary switched the subject. "It was bad luck on him Mr Sheridan was dead. But he thinks if he can get a licence he might take up peddling."

"Peddling, is it?" said her father with disgust. "He could have been a pedlar in Ireland."

"Maybe over there is some people with money to buy."

He did not answer that, and Mary got bolder.

"He says that if he had me with him he is sure he would do better for himself."

"Oh? And tell me why is that?"

"He would have me to look after his washing and his clothes."

"Oh, is that it?"

"And he would be more at peace in his mind."

"Would he now? In his mind?"

Then it was Mary who did not answer, red with embarrassment and anger. Her father spoke more gently.

"Why are all of you in such a hurry to leave your country?"

"What else is there to do? I might as well be buried as to stay."

"Well, and if you are," her father said, "you're buried in your own land. Do you know what they call the boats? The floating coffins, they call them, because there's so many dies of the fever on the way across."

"Anyone can die," said Mary. "You can die of the fever even if you never leave Ireland."

At night in the bunkhouse in the middle of a forest blacker, thicker than anything he could have imagined, with the men around him playing cards and working on their boots and clothing, one fellow fiddling with a Jew's-harp, James was writing to Mary.

I have got a job now, Mary, working on a road that is being built from Brantford to London. There is a London, too, in Canada West. It is hard work but I am fit for it, more than I was. There is as much meat as you can eat here, and I have put on nearly a stone in weight since you saw me last.

When we get all the trees cut down, there will be tidy roads and farms and towns as comfortable as anybody could want, and I tell you, Mary, this is a better place for you and me to live and raise our family than at home. Over here the hired man sits down to eat with the family and if a man will work he can make his way...

While he wrote he was listening to a conversation next to him. Some others were listening as well.

"And where would that have happened? Do ye know?"

"I don't know the name of the place, but it was down east of here. The wages didn't come and they didn't come, so they put down their axes. They said they wouldn't work no more."

"They said they wouldn't work no more till the wages come?"

"They said that. And they wouldn't."

"And did the wages come then?"

"No. It was the military come."

The man with the Jew's-harp spoke up now.

"I hear some places they never seen their wages for six weeks."

"It was longer. It was months."

"And them without a penny to send to their families that was waiting on it, and them starving."

"Why didn't they do something about it then?"

"What can they do? Raise a fuss and in comes the military and they end up going to jail. Then they write it up in the paper and they call it a riot. They never call it a strike, they call it a riot. They always say it was the drink done it; they never mention the wages."

"Well. They say our wages'll be here by the end of the week."

"So they better. Or might be a couple of heads broke."

"Who is going to break the heads of a pack of soldiers with guns?" said James, not meaning to start a fight and, in fact, thinking with affection of his old gun at home, his father's pistol. What a fool he had been not to bring it.

A man got up off his bunk. "We could, if we was all the right kind of Irishmen."

"Is it Orangemen you mean?" said James, getting up too, partly amazed at his own readiness.

"I said what I mean."

Then what would have happened God knows, but the man with the Jew's-harp began to play a song they knew, and the man who had told about the wages said they should have sense, the both of them, if there was more fights they would all get their pay docked. James went back to where he had written *"if a man will work he can make his way,"* and wrote further.

There is Orangemen working in this gang too but I will try all I can to keep clear of trouble. Mary, I know it is asking you to go against your father's wish but I tell you again here is the best place for us. And for me, I know I cannot stay any place *unless you are with me. Anything I can do to make your life happy, believe me I will do it and it is only you I can love till I am dead.*

When he had written this, he put his head in his hands and then roused himself, looked at the men around him.

If you come could you remember to bring the gun.

Mary was writing, too, in the sitting room of her father's house, with her father and her sister in the room as usual, the children asleep. Her father pretended to read, her sister had been crying. They seemed to Mary already small and fixed and distant like pictures she would carry in her mind, and the room she knew so well had become, though she was still in it, a room in her memory.

We have booked our passage, James, on the ship Northumberland *out of Belfast bound for Quebec. Annie gets free but little James is charged half fare. Father has paid our passage for he saw I would break my heart if I did not go. I pray you will be waiting for us in Quebec, but if anything should happen that you are not there I will go on to my sister Elsie that is near Chatham as you know in Canada West, and you can come for me there. Oh, James, what a lot of things we will have to say to each other when we meet. I think every minute of it, and what it will be like to see you again.*

Dearest James, I pray you do not fail to meet us at Quebec.

She dipped her pen and saw her father watching her and felt as if she had just seen the edge of something she couldn't afford to look at (was it absence, was it death, was it final loss?), and wrote on.

In Montreal, two weeks before Mary's ship was due to land at Quebec, James went to the premises of a Mr McConnell, a ship's chandler, a man whose name had been given him by one of the workers on the road. He meant to get a few days' work loading, or in the warehouse. He was saving all he could against the time when Mary and the children would be with him. He was afraid she would be disappointed, the country might not look as promising to her as he had made it seem in his letters, nor his prospects so bright. But he was sure to find something, and it was true that chances were far better here. Luck must be running with him, since he had been granted the great luck of her coming.

McConnell was a sour-looking fellow. He got up from his bookkeeper's table to ask what James wanted.

"A job, sir."

"And doesn't everybody?"

"I've been in trade, sir."

"It's no matter to me whether you've been in trade or not. And don't tell me you're an Irishman, for that's no matter to me either. I'm an Irishman myself."

"Yes, sir," said James, meaning it was not a thing anybody could mistake.

"I'm an Irishman myself and I do all I can for the Irish. I hire them when I can, and I send them where there's work if I know about. And I've given them money out of my own pocket. But they keep landing here boatload after boatload and there's a limit to the number a man can take care of. Two men for every job now, and they're turning them back from the States. They get off the boats starving."

"Yes, sir. I wouldn't be staying. I'm a hard worker. I worked in the bush."

"I can see them coming up from the boats and I can smell them, too, when the wind's in the right direction. I say that and I'm an Irishman."

"I'm just on my way to Quebec to meet my wife's boat that's due in a fortnight. I only hoped I could pick up a little work on the way, if you needed a strong man for loading or anything else—"

He felt a cramp in his stomach. Most likely it was hunger. He had stuffed himself before he left the road camp, then tried to go easy on eating, to save his money.

"You're bringing a wife over?" said McConnell sternly.

"And my two children that were born in Ireland," said James, who had already given up hope and turned towards the door.

"Can you write a letter?"

"Yes, I can."

"You can spend a fortnight doing some letters and accounts for me, for it's a terrible time I'm having collecting the money that's owed to me. I can't afford to pay you but I will, so you'll have some silver in your pocket when you meet your wife in Quebec."

"I'm obliged to you."

"Come behind here and I'll show you what to do."

James lifted the moveable part of the counter and felt a shocking weakness. It seemed as if it could not be part of him at all, it could not be James who felt weak. He thought of Mary at sea and wondered if she could be suffering sickness at that moment. But he had faith that she was on a healthy ship, a decent ship, not like his. Her father would have seen to it.

McConnell looked at him closely. "When did you eat last?"

"Yesterday."

"More likely the day before, by the looks of you. Come with me, come with me. The books'll wait."

At first Mary could not think what to do, but sit on the porch of Elsie's house and look along the road. She would have some work on her lap that she could do without thinking; she could sew the whole seam of a flannel sheet without knowing how she began or ended it.

Her ears got so sharp she could hear a horse long before it was in sight, and she even thought sometimes she could hear a man walking, where logs were laid over wet places in the road. It was Elsie who thought to write to Montreal, to a Mr Warren, who was a friend of their father's. James had written that he would go through Montreal and might find work there on his way.

Elsie would not say what Mary knew she was thinking, which was that James was not reliable, that he thought himself too good for farming, that he used to like his drink.

Everyone was kind. Elsie's husband went in to town nearly every other day, to see if there was any mail. When he did not go, their neighbour sometimes went. His name was Henry Norris, and he, too, was sorry for Mary in her trouble. When he had to tell her there was no letter, his eyes looked to her like an old dog's.

"Thank you just the same, Mr Norris," Mary said, but she could not stay to hear him talking with Elsie, all about everyday things, that there were so many people on the streets in town you would think they had nothing else to do, and that there was not the colour of thread Elsie wanted available, and that there was likely to be a long fall this year and an open winter. Mary would leave them talking and go to watch young James playing with Elsie's children, or walk farther, to stand hemmed in by the heavy woods, the raw dirt roads, the fields full of charred stumps. Whatever was she doing in this country if James was not with her?

The day Elsie's husband brought the letter Mary knew he had it by the sound of the horse's hoofs, from a long way off. She was taking up cabbages down in the garden, and she heard the hoofs and ran, and Elsie came running, too, out of the house, looking so glad that Mary forgave her anything she had been thinking. Elsie's husband, too, with his thin face and his big ears, who had once seemed to Mary a terribly ugly man for her sister to marry, looked lovely to her now, with the expression of triumph and relief he had as he handed her the letter. She stood with her back to them, to read it.

Of course she ought to have seen at once that the writing on the envelope was not James', but she was so sure that she was getting word from James – it was just like all the times in Ireland when she had waited and waited and at last the letter came – that she tore it open, and read the "Dear Mrs Thompson," and read the whole letter to the end – it was not very long – with a feeling of joy still warming her from her feet up. So strong and sure was the feeling that she could not take in what the letter said; it seemed she had mistaken the words in it, and she read it through again, thinking that the words must change, for

the message in the letter made no sense. She could not be as happy as she was if James was dead, and how was it possible, for James to be dead?

She read it very slowly, word by word. She made herself understand what it said. It said that James was dead. He had been working for a Mr McConnell, in Montreal. He was hired for a fortnight's work in September. The first day he was at work he took sick, and he was taken to hospital, and he died there. He died of cholera. He was dead. He had been dead before she landed at Quebec. He had died in Montreal, in a hospital. She had taken the steamer, from Quebec, she had landed in Montreal and that was where she got the stage, the first stage. She could hardly remember anything about that, except that she had been sure, in every crowd, that she would see James hurrying towards her. He had been there such a short time before her, in Montreal. But when she was there, he was dead. He was already dead.

Mr Warren said that he had gone to the place where James had been staying, he had found that out from Mr McConnell, and he had seen James' bag there, they were still keeping it. There was a packet of letters in it that he took the liberty of glancing at. They were Mary's letters, written from Ireland. He said that he would send them along to her, and that he begged her pardon for his bad news.

Mary turned and saw them waiting and knew she would have to tell them. It was immensely hard for her to say the words; it was a pain to get them out, and seemed like treachery, as if she herself saying them finally made them true.

She went into the church sometimes, not to pray really but to be by herself, away from them always watching her and being good to her and respectfully trying to cheer her up. She thought she would cry in the church, with nobody to see her, but when she got there, she found she couldn't. She knelt for a while and said some prayers without caring what she said, and then she just sat. It was a poor new church, you could still smell the lumber.

On a Saturday Henry Norris came in and sat in the pew across from her, but one behind, as if he wouldn't be so bold as to sit directly opposite. He always looked as if he suffered for her, and this day he looked it so plainly that she was pitying him, and asked him were there many people in town. Then he could say what he liked to say.

"There was so many there you would think they had nothing else to do."

How old was he – forty, fifty? She could not tell those ages. He had some of a bachelor's fussy ways, but he was kind looking.

"You've never seen my house, Mrs Thompson."

Why should she care about his house? She thought he was trying to distract her, as the others did, and she had to let him.

"It's as big as your sister's place but it seems bigger, when I'm all alone in it. I was thinking I'd put up a frame house in a year or two."

Mary nodded politely, as if his plans interested her.

"I've got a hundred acres, the same as your brother-in-law. I've a good spring and a good wood lot. On a place like mine you can raise nearly everything you need. You just have to buy the sugar and the tea. You need never go hungry."

She could not think of any remark to make, and after a moment he said fearfully but determinedly, "Will you come and see my house, then? When will you come?"

That was the first she understood what he was really saying to her, and her answer started before she understood it, so she had to keep on.

"I could come and see it – I could come next Sunday."

He got up briskly as if his business was finished, crossed himself in a satisfied way, and went out.

"It might be you could do worse than to marry him," Elsie said. "He's a good man. He's a sober man."

"What else could he be, at his age?" said Mary in a flash. She would often see an insult to James where none was intended.

"It's not up to me, though," said Elsie coolly. "You must please yourself."

"I know very well you cannot keep us here much longer."

"I never said a word of that! You shall stay here as long as it suits you."

"You and Thomas have enough of your own to look after."

They were at the clothes-line, hanging the clean clothes out to dry. Mary held a sheet against her face.

"I think and think about it," she said. "I think about the children."

"Never mind," said Elsie, speaking remorsefully now. "Never mind, Mary, you must please yourself. If you don't want to, you can stay with us over the winter, and we will write to father, and he will get the money somehow, and next summer you can go home."

Mary shook her head against the sheet. She remembered the ship, the heaving ocean, and how she and the baby were sick together and she thought they would die and leave young James to wander on deck with no one to care for him, to starve or be washed over.

"I could never face that voyage again."

Over at the wood pile, Henry Norris was splitting logs, with Elsie's husband. Mary took the sheet away from her face and looked at him. He was strong still, with the axe. He was gentle with her children. He would be good to them even when he had his own children, because he was a just man. The wedding ring she wore had been loose on her finger for a long time. It was easy to slide it off, into her apron pocket.

Her name would be Mary Norris. She would stay here, she would die here. She would change from the person she was into someone she could not imagine, another man's wife, and she would put those letters away where she could not look at them until she was old, so old they couldn't trouble her, and with so much life between her and them she would read them like a story.

The Danes

Although Norway, Denmark, Sweden, and Iceland are now among the most prosperous and peaceful countries in the world, they were not always so. At various times in their histories, war, depression, and natural disasters have forced Scandinavians to emigrate. Between 1870 and 1901, for example, nearly one-fifth of the Icelandic population emigrated to North America, many settling in Manitoba and northern Ontario. They left, in part, because a terrible earthquake destroyed much of the country and precipitated a major economic depression.

In Denmark, arable land was scarce and had been divided into small farms. Thus, many farmers could hope to be no more than tenants, or, at most, farm managers. Emigration offered them the chance to be land-owners themselves. Other Danish emigrants, tradesmen and skilled workers particularly, sought the opportunity to set up independent businesses. Still others left their homes because of a natural Scandinavian affinity for the sea or a simple love of adventure.

For the Scandinavian immigrants to Canada success often depended on where they settled as well as when they came. In spite of the availability of land, economic depressions also hit Canada. Industrial growth in this country resulted in worker exploitation and in an inability to gather sufficient funds to move west, or indeed to move anywhere. For the Scandinavians, coming from highly developed countries, life in Canada was difficult indeed. Some saw future opportunities, while others were disappointed – often immigration had not only failed to better their lives, it had actually lowered their standard of living.

In 1911, 1912, and 1913, there was considerable prejudice against the immigrants from Scandinavia: they came as trained workers to areas where poverty and lack of skills had forced the local populace into poorly paid jobs. The newcomers posed an economic threat to the residents. In addition, the Scandinavian languages sounded like German to untrained ears, and Europe was on the verge of the First World War.

Scandinavians who came with money were able to buy farms and set up businesses; those who came with factory skills soon found work in growing industries. But those unfortunate few who came without money and who hoped to obtain crown lands were disappointed and did not, for another generation, know success.

1911

Many Danes left a country that was, for some, comfortable and tidy to go to one that must have seemed totally uncivilized. In spite of the profound optimism that caused them to leave a sheltered way of life in favour of a strange new one, some must have missed the tried and familiar, and harboured doubts about the wisdom of their move. The change was perhaps hardest for the women, who often had the most to lose and the least to gain from the move.

They travelled
by many modes
through a
strange land
to an unknown future

Bits and pieces of Denmark were all
they could carry with them.
They had to be as practical as possible,
but a few tokens of remembrance,
of the old life, were necessary, too –
a little sad magic to gaze upon
when the doubts and longing grew.
No matter how complete the physical break
with the past might be, some part
of the soul always stays at home.
The second generation knows no other life,
but the first generation remains
divided between two worlds.

Children of a new land

What must the children have thought? Through all these changes, the children were the inarticulate, the unconsulted ones. How often did they know what their parents' hopeful explanations meant? What fears and fantasies did they have in this strange and crude world, as the place of their birth faded into a land out of storybooks rather than memory?

One man – one town

Having founded the only business in an area, a man could become virtual owner of the town that grew up dependent on his industry. He provided everything – housing, stores, schooling. In return, the townspeople built his roads, hauled his logs, ran his mills, and blasted the path for his railway. They also lived in his houses, and bought provisions at his store.

The gulf between
rich and poor
was hard to bridge

As the family grew,
debts often increased.
There were more mouths
to feed, more clothes to
be bought. Although the
basics were always
available, only the owner
of the town, his managers,
and a fortunate few were
guaranteed the luxuries
that come with position.

In moments of despair, the few carefully preserved artifacts from Denmark provided consolation with memories and bittersweet recollections of original dreams.

Yet hope remained.

A Long Hard Walk

TIMOTHY FINDLEY

August 1911

I hate this place. I don't know where I am. I look at maps and cannot find myself.

Hans keeps telling me everything will be all right. How can anything be all right until we leave this place and go back home? Home. To Denmark.

We have walked along this road for hours. Since dawn. The driver keeps saying, "*Vite! Vite! Faites vite!*" He's French. How can I like him? He frightens me. He beats the horse. Half the time he mumbles English, half the time he's shouting French. "*Vite! Vite! Vite!*" I want to hear Danish. Danish.

My thighs ache. My eyes burn. My mouth is full of dust. I want to sit down. Stop and drink water. The air is not even air. We are walking through a furnace. Dry. Not a cloud. No wind. Not even a breeze. And the sound of cicadas. Screaming.

Canada! New Brunswick! Hah!

Hans walks ahead of me, calling back that soon we will be there. He's lying, of course. There isn't anywhere to come to. The whole of this journey, starting in Denmark, has just been one long lie. "*We will go to America*" – we've come to Canada. "*I have a job in Little Falls, New York*" – it lasted a week. "*We will live in a house of our own*" – a lean-to with a roof that leaked. "*You will be with other Danes*" – there were just Germans. "*We are going home*" – what home? Home is Denmark. "*It's only for a week or so, until I find my brother Nels*" – Nels is dead. I know it. No one has heard from Nels for over a year.

The road has wound us up to a high plateau. There are hills stretching for miles. I cannot see the end. Tall yellow grass, so dry it breaks in your fingers. Clouds of grasshoppers – locusts: I don't know which. And small, pale moths that stick in your throat.

The cart has broken down. I'm sitting here waiting. Hans and the driver cannot communicate. Hans' English and the driver's do not seem to be the same language. They broke my rocking chair. It fell from the back of the cart on the hill and the cow has walked on it. Now all the spindles which my father carved are smashed – every one of them. So I've made Hans take down my trunk while they fix the cart. All my china. All my linen. Papa's clock. Mama's plates. I will kill that driver if they're broken. Him and Hans. And that damn cow.

Hans is smiling at me now. He call this "adventure."

No one in their right mind would come here to

live. Look at it. Look! It's nothing but a burnt-out steppe covered with scruff and crawling with insects – like a head with lice. And I itch. My dress is saturated with dust, and where I sweat, it turns to mud. I smell like an animal. I might as well roll in the dirt. And howl. But here I sit – Rosamund Jensen – holding my chipped enamelled mug of tea, with my apron thrown across my head to ward off the sun.

I don't know where I am, only where I've been. And I want to go back. Denmark – where my clothes were clean and white and the marketplace was filled with vegetables and fish. Here I am because I married Hans and wives must go where husbands lead. Like cows. Tied up with ropes to the backs of broken-down carts – stumbling over the fallen remnants of the past.

No. I cannot stay here. I will not stay.

September 1911

We have come to a farm colony they call New Denmark. Let them call it what they will, it's nothing at all like home. Except for the language. They do speak Danish here. But for how long? Many of the children talk to one another in English. *Assimilate.* That is the new big word. *Assimilate.* I don't know what it means.

The first Danes came here in 1871. Forty years ago. Then there were seven families and ten bachelors. Now, perhaps two hundred people. They don't look like Danes anymore. They just look tired. And poor. And dirty. The children run around barefoot. Like savages. Danes should wear shoes.

When we rounded the bend in the road and I saw that the houses were near I insisted they stop the cart and let me climb up on the seat. I was not going to walk into any place where there were Danes and let them see me limping along behind the cow. I even put on my other dress and a clean white apron.

The road was full of dogs and children. Not that you could really call it a road. It was the same old ruts we'd been on for days, only now there were houses on either side. To Hans, of course, it was paradise. He kept on waving at everyone, calling out and laughing. "Hello! Hello! My name is Hans Jensen and I come from Denmark!" Why did he have to advertise? He looked like a Prussian beggar.

Here they are farmers. This is a source of great excitement to Hans, being a farmer himself. He doesn't see the holes in the road, the dust. He doesn't see that the fields are full of rocks and stumps. He only sees the blooming farmland no one here will realize for ten or fifteen years. If he saw one geranium, Hans would come home and say, "I saw a garden, today." He looks around at the clearings and he says to me, "Rosamund, how could anyone ask for more than a bit of land like this?" Then he sighs, and smiles that private smile I hate, because it shuts me out. "Adam was a man after my own heart," he says. And I want to kick him. As if he alone belonged in Eden! Where does he think the rest of us dream of living?

Down the road, we come to the house they've told us belongs to Nels. Lord God in Heaven. Nels had written to say he was farming. Then to say he was married. Then to say there was a child. After which – silence. Now here it is. His "farm."

The house is unbearably small with only a loft to sleep in. The walls are unpainted. The yard hasn't even flowers. It smells of dust and cabbage soup.

Hans says, "Get down."

I say, "No." I know that to get down here is to stay.

Then Marghrita comes out carrying a baby. She puts her hand above her eyes to shade them from the sun. Three more children emerge and stand behind her. Then a dog.

When Marghrita speaks she says, "Who's there?" In English.

Hans says to me again, "Get down," but I won't. Then he says to Marghrita, "I am Hans Jensen. If you are Marghrita Jensen, then I am your husband's brother."

She says, "Yes," still in English, "I am Marghrita Jensen. Why are you here?"

Why are you here? It almost makes me love her.

Hans explains we had thought to settle in America and how that hasn't worked out, so now we are on our way home; but first we have come to see his brother. We've even brought him a cow for his farm.

Marghrita says, "What farm? There is no farm."

I laugh.

Hans says one last time, "Get down," and now I do, because I know it's safe. I know that any minute, Marghrita will tell us Nels has died, and the farm and the happiness he'd written about were all lies. Later, eating the cabbage soup, she will tell us her plans to go back home and then we can truly rejoice. We will go back together. To Denmark.

We come inside. We drink Aquavit standing on the mud floor – toasting our arrival, toasting our meeting with this long-lost relative. Toasting our departure. "*Sköl! Sköl! Sköl!*"

Then Marghrita says, "Nels would be here, of course, but he's cutting down trees. For the railroad."

My heart sinks. Nels is alive. Not that I wish him ill, but there will be no rejoicing now. We will not go back together. Maybe no one will ever go back.

Later, when Hans has gone outside to look at the sun, Marghrita says, "You wonder why I don't speak Danish, don't you? Me and my children.

Well, my father wonders, too. But Nels says we live here, now. This is where we are."

I cannot look at her. She makes me want to weep. Yes, I am thinking. Yes. You are here. And you will never escape. Neither you nor your children. And your children, God help them, will never be civilized. They will never wear shoes. They will never be Danish. This is the meaning of *assimilate*. To forget who you are.

Hans went off through the forest. Eighteen miles to the railroad and Nels. He was gone for two days. Now we are lying here in this attic in a house that is owned by Mrs Jeppesen. There isn't even room in Marghrita's house to put us up. Mrs Jeppesen, who is a widow without children is glad to have us stay with her and use her loft. And pay rent. I don't really blame her, asking us for money. She is poor. With the drought, the land will not produce, and the men have mostly gone away and left their farms to work on the railroad. In the winter they go to the lumber camps. Whenever they are home, they lie with their wives so there will be more children. And now I'm lying here with Hans and he is saying, "We will stay."

"But you promised," I remind him.

"There will be no argument," he says.

"But there *is* argument. *I* am arguing."

"Nevertheless, we are staying."

I get out of bed.

"Now what?" he says.

I tell him I will not make babies for Canadians.

"Who's making babies? I am tired. Get back in bed."

"No," I tell him. "No. You promised. And I mean to hold you to your promise. We are going *home*."

Silence. Then he says, "All right. I promise. We will only stay till I've made enough money to pay for our passage."

"And how will you make this money then, to pay for our passage home?"

He explains there is a job in a town twenty

miles away from here. Henley Point. I ask him why, if there's a job in a town that's only twenty miles away, Nels or one of the other men in New Denmark doesn't accept it?

Hans does not answer.

"Why?" I ask him. "Why? What can be wrong with this job, that no one here will accept it?"

But he will not tell me. I will have to wait and discover that for myself. So I will sit in this chair, wearing my socks, with my shawl and my great coat around me. And I will not go back to his bed. Why should I have his babies? Babies will entrap me. That's what he wants. To entrap me in this dreadful place forever, speaking English and raising his children as foreigners. No. I will have no foreigners. Only Danes.

October 1911

What is wrong with the job is Mr McLeod. Mr McLeod is the owner of the "McLeod Lumber Company: Henley Point, New Brunswick." This is what is written over the gates, but it might as well be written on the forehead of every man who works here. Maybe on the foreheads of their wives and children, too. People have called this place a "company town," but it's not. It's a one-man town. Mr McLeod owns it all. And us.

Hans is working for him now. Clearing land. Burning stumps. In the spring, they will plant hay to feed the horses that will pull the logs that will feed the mill. Mr McLeod drives an automobile, the largest I have seen. It makes a good deal of noise – and this seems appropriate. Everywhere it goes, it scares the horses. Then it stops and Mr McLeod steps down. Everyone stands around cowed and silent. There's a man called Travis who rides on the running board. He's supposed to be a foreman at the mill. But he's hardly ever away from Mr McLeod's side.

Mr McLeod owns the lumber yard, the mill, the store, and all the houses in town. There are no police. There is only Mr Travis. Mr McLeod is the judge, in command of every life. There's only one kind of crime – drunkenness. Mr McLeod passes sentence, and the sentence is always the same: you lose your job, your money, and your house. Then he runs you out of town. Or Mr Travis does.

In the church, at funerals, when Reverend Mr Macdougal rises and says, "The Lord giveth and the Lord taketh away," everyone looks at Mr McLeod. *Lord Donald McLeod.*

We live upstairs above the Stuarts. The house smells like a barn. Mrs Stuart's children have a dog. He lifts his leg in the hallway. I have spoken to the Stuart's son, Sandy. He doesn't seem to understand that the dog should not do this. But the girl is more civilized. Her name is Alexandra. On the day we moved in, she brought me a handful of daisies. I cannot be tempted into making friends – not here – but I smile at her and she smiles back. There's a hole in the middle of the floor which Hans has not mended yet. I cover it with a chair. One day, through the hole, I heard Mrs Stuart saying to Alexandra, "Don't you go puttin' on airs like that German bitch upstairs."

We live in two small rooms. The smaller one we use for a bedroom, sleeping on the floor. We have a mattress, but no bed. The other room must serve as kitchen, bathroom and dining room. I try to keep it clean. I wash the floor. I scrub it with a brush. But the dust comes in from the mill and even settles in the bureau drawers. This is the very first home that Hans and I have ever had, but I will not set my things out here.

The very first day – the day that Alexandra brought me flowers – I opened my trunk and got out papa's clock and mama's plates and all the linen I'd embroidered for my trousseau. Then I put it all away. Even the caps I so long to wear to keep my hair clean. I will never bring them out again. They break my heart. They smell of home.

The people who live next door play music on a gramophone. This is a machine you turn with a handle, and out comes an orchestra, or someone singing. I have never seen it, except at a distance through their window.

Everything I see, these days, is seen at a distance. Even Hans, who works all day beyond the town and always comes home through the dark.

Way off – under the forest up the hill – they are blowing everything up. Tree stumps and rocks. After the dynamite, they set the trees on fire. All day long the air is full of smoke and all night long the sky is red and yellow. Chains of smoke go up across the sun. The light is a copper colour.

Morning and afternoon, the geese fly south. They never settle here. The fire must drive them off. Mrs Stuart says we are missing a feast since the men cannot go out and shoot them as they pass. I would rather have their wings to fly away.

Sometimes I walk by the river, after my work is done and the wash is boiling in the yard. I look around and I think – it could be pretty here. If it weren't for the noise from the mill and the smoke from the fires. They will soon be done with the burning, and then I am hoping Hans will come and say that we have money enough to go to Massachusetts or New York. The only ships sailing before winter are ships for Italy and Spain. Imagine! We will land at Barcelona in the sun! Geese! Lend me your wings! Dance! Gramophone music! We are going home! The long walk is over!

November 1911

Tonight, when Hans came back, I made him a bath in the big iron tub. We laughed, because we said it would fall through the floor and land in Mrs Stuart's kitchen. Hans' clothes will smell of fire for the last time tonight. The rains have started, drenching the fields to mud. The sky is full of golden leaves. And red. I got the water for Hans' bath by drawing in the eaves and running the rain into pails, which I heated on the stove. By the time I poured the bath I saw, too late, the leaves had come down into the pails and were floating around his knees.

"They look like boats," I said, but he didn't take the hint. I want it to come from him. I want him to be the one who says it first: *Rosamund, we are going home*. But I shall make him say it tonight. In bed.

The rooms are warm. The windows shut. I have made a big stew. And bread. I have brought out our only bottle of Aquavit, saved in my trunk for celebrations. Real Danish Aquavit. I have put it with the candles by the bed. And two small cups. Hans does not know this yet. He is sitting, smoking his pipe, with his eyes half closed. Perhaps he is trying to think of some nice way of telling me. Maybe he will show me the money. Shower me with it. Throw it in the air for me to catch and count. Maybe he already has our passage. Later, he will show me a letter telling us the name of our ship and the port from which we sail.

We rise. I am leading the way. I put down the lamp and blow it out. I have put my clothes on the chair. I pull my nightgown over my head. I can feel it touch the floor. It is heavy. My toes are cold. I laugh. We usually sleep in our socks, but not tonight. I kneel beside the mattress, putting out my hands to find my way. The dark is very dark and I want to light the candles. I have brought my shawl so we can sit up, backs against the wall, and drink the Aquavit. Celebrate. Make love. Beneath the covers, I discover Hans is naked. Not even wearing drawers. As I find my place and am searching for my shawl, he rolls on his side and places his leg across my thighs.

"Wait," I am saying. "Wait. Let me light the candles." I am fumbling for the matches. Hans has put his hand beneath the back of my gown and is reaching up, his arm encircling me. His fingers touch my breast from underneath. "Wait. Wait. Wait!" I am saying. Laughing. And he kisses my shoulder just as I find the matches. There! I have struck one.

Light.
I touch both candles with the flame.
Everything stops.

Hans says, "What have you done? You must be mad!"

He removes his hand from my breast and his lips from my shoulder. He is sitting up, pulling away from me. I feel the rush of cold as he leaves the bed.

"What is the matter?" I ask him.

Hans has come round the bed and is reaching down through the candlelight.

"What is *wrong*?" I say to him.

"This," he says, and he shows me the bottle of Aquavit. "What are you doing with this?"

I tell him we will celebrate.

"Celebrate what?" he yells at me, marching naked towards the kitchen sink. "Celebrate that I should lose my job?"

"Your job! Your job? You have no job. The fires are over. All the burning's done. There is no job."

Hans is pouring Aquavit down the sink. I run up behind him with the candle.

"Stop that!" I scream at him. "Stop that! Stop!" It is the only Aquavit we have. It comes from Denmark. It is precious. Every drop is precious. "*Stop!*"

We struggle for the bottle. The candle falls and goes out. We struggle in the darkness. Then the bottle is broken.

I begin to weep.

Hans cannot find the matches. He stumbles across the floor and falls. His naked leg sticks down through the hole into Mrs Stuart's kitchen. I can hear their dog begin to bark. My weeping turns to laughter.

Hans says, "Bring me a light!" But I cannot. How can I move? I am laughing too hard.

Downstairs Mrs Stuart is screaming, "Don't look, Alexandra! Go in the other room!" My husband's naked leg is dangling from their ceiling. Mrs Stuart hits it with a broom. I have never laughed so hard in all my life. Hans is furious.

Now it is very late, and we are lying here again in the bed.

"Why did you pour the Aquavit down the sink?"

"I have promised Mr McLeod. There will be no liquor."

I am astounded. "How can you promise such a thing? Aquavit is our custom."

"Not any more."

"We are Danes!" I yell at him, rising to my feet. I am so angry I could hit him. "We are Danes! It is our custom!"

"Not anymore," he says. "There will be no liquor."

There is silence. Then I am saying, "What are you saying?"

Hans says, "We are staying here. I have a job."

We are staying here. He has a job.

My life is over.

December 1911

Sometimes I am nearly ill with loneliness. I keep a pail nearby. When I think I am going to be sick I kneel above the pail and wait, but nothing happens. All I do is retch. Today I have scrubbed the floor three times because I was on my knees from dawn and could not rise. Hans is gone from morning to night. He is making a barn. For Mr McLeod.

Mr McLeod. Mr McLeod keeps us in this house – the only house, he says, he has to offer us. My trunk is still unpacked. I have no friends. *No one to talk to!* No one to help me escape.

But I am saving money in a jar. One day I will have enough to buy my ticket to Halifax. Hans will not know of this. Not until it is time for me to go. I hide the jar where I know he will never look, inside the ceiling over our heads. I have now fifty cents, five dollars. Five new dollar bills and fifty cents in dimes. The dimes make hardly any noise. I exchange my pennies for them at the store. Miss Proudfoot says I am a good cash-paying customer. What she does not know is that if I did not pay with cash I would not have change to hide. Credit will not buy my ticket home.

Soon Hans will be an Odd Person. Thursday nights he wears his suit and walks across the town to the Odd Persons' Hall and looks important. Now I have to give him a clean white shirt and press his trousers twice a week because he also goes to church on Sundays.

Sundays are dreadful. Dreadful. Hans insists that we go to the foreign church. Presbyterians. And we have to sit near the front so Mr McLeod will be certain to remark that we are there. Sometimes I think that Mr McLeod writes the sermons. Every Sunday, Reverend Mr Macdougal lectures us upon work and alcoholic beverages. And sin. Sin is not being grateful for being here. Not being grateful for the roofs above our heads and the sausage that we eat. Not being glad for the sound of the mill. Sin is burning candles after ten PM. Sin is not being exhausted. Mr McLeod smiles and nods and one day I will trip him in the aisle.

Today the sun is shining and the snow is crisp and blue on the hills. After Hans has gone to work I put on my overcoat and woollen hat and rubber boots and walk off down the street to look in the windows of Miss Proudfoot's store. Miss Proudfoot does not own the store, of course. The store is Mr McLeod's, but she runs it for him and it says she is Proprietress above the door and Manageress above her desk. She has a very happy smile. Sometimes I watch her through the window. I never go inside unless it is Friday night. Other ladies spend whole days inside Miss Proudfoot's store. They talk and stand about between the counters, stealing spools of thread and pairs of scissors. I have seen this stealing through the windows. But I never go inside myself unless it's Friday night.

Not until today, this morning, which is Tuesday. Christmas is just a week away. Next Monday. I am to buy for Hans two pairs of socks and a scarf. I have knitted gloves for him already. He is to buy a blouse for me which I have chosen from a book. White, on which I will embroider blue.

When I go inside a bell rings over my head. Two other ladies are present, poking around and most likely stealing things. Miss Proudfoot must be somewhere in the back. I cannot see her anywhere. The other ladies turn away as soon as I come in. One of them is Mrs Morgan, who is Welsh and cozies up to all the Scottish ladies so she won't feel alone. When she speaks she has an accent not unlike my own and sometimes I wonder whether Mrs Morgan isn't Dutch or German, masquerading in the English language. People who steal thread have no pride and will pretend to anything.

Who the other lady is I do not know and do not care. I smile at them and that is all that I can do. And so they turn away and whisper and I hear them saying things like, "Mrs Stuart says . . ." and "Doesn't care for her husband. . . ." Let them. I am me and that is all I am and won't pretend otherwise.

After a minute I can hear them leave and then I am standing there alone. I close my eyes. Cloth and clothing, tea and coffee fill my nostrils. Then I am startled by Miss Proudfoot saying to me, "Can I help you, Mrs Jensen?"

"No." I am embarrassed. She has seen my face. And my tears. But she is good to me. She smiles.

"I can see you like the smell of this store as much as I do, Mrs Jensen," she says.

"Yes," I am telling her, looking for a handkerchief. Can it be that I have come out without one?

"These are very nice," she says and shows me a shelf that is filled with Irish linen. "The thing is," she says, and holds up a small square handkerchief untrimmed, "I have discovered one or two unfinished ones and I am putting them on sale for a matter of pennies."

"Thank you," I say, and accept it.

"Yes," says Miss Proudfoot, while I blow my nose, "this store and its smells are very comforting to me. My father owned a store like this at home. In Ecclefechin."

"Yes. Yes," I say. "And my father, too, when I was a girl in Vibörg." Now, my father manages an inn, but I do not tell her that. Stores are what we have in common.

Miss Proudfoot takes my money. And then she says to me, "I've made a pot of tea. I'd rather drink it with some company."

This is my first invitation since I came to North America. I realize the implication. Now, I must ask her to my house. But I will. She will understand. She will not expect to find a tea cloth on my table.

February 1912

Agh! This country! Now it rains. And yesterday it snowed. Tomorrow it could blaze with flames for all I know.

They call this mud the "January thaw." In *February*. Everyone here is crazy. Nobody thinks beforehand what they do. The hill behind the town, where all last year they cut the trees and pulled the stumps, has come cascading down across the fields and heads toward the river like a batter spilling from a bowl.

No one has been paid a cent these last two weeks. All except Hans and the men he works with where they build the barn have been laid off because the mill is closed. Mr McLeod says it is not his fault the rain comes down. Reverend Mr Macdougal prays on Sundays now for the drought they had last summer. All of the men are restless and at home. Next door, the gramophone is louder every minute, playing sometimes nearly all night long. I am afraid for Mrs Bailey and her children who are living there.

Hans has told me Mr Bailey drinks in secret. Sometimes Mr Bailey shouts and the sound of the music rises, even through the rain, to drown him out. I have watched through their windows and I see what happens. Mrs Bailey makes the children turn the handle faster and faster. Then she makes the volume loud, and everybody sings to cover up the noise that Mr Bailey makes with his shouting. Poor Mrs Bailey. She is so afraid. If her husband loses his job they will be made to leave Henley Point and there is nowhere else to go. What I am hoping is that Mrs Bailey has a jar like me in which she keeps some money for escape. But no. They are not like that. They spend all the money they have on music and drink. Music and drink are the only journeys they will ever make.

This is the night Hans goes to become an Odd

Person. All winter long he has attended with them in their hall. Now he will be a member. None of it makes any sense to me. All these men dress up in their suits and go down there and stand around and speechify at one another. Hans says being a member is an honour. I say it is just a good excuse to get away from being locked up in here. Like me. Odd Persons. Why must they call themselves that? Now he tells me it is not Odd Persons but Odd Fellows. Does he think there is a difference?

Tonight, before he leaves, he says to me that Mr McLeod likes the work he's done in putting up the barn. Barn. Barn. Barn. It's all he ever talks about. He says Mr McLeod will soon offer him the job of farm manager. In charge of all the horses and the pigsties!

"Tell him you already have a pigsty here," I say to him. "Who needs another?"

Hans turn white. He is afraid of anger.

"Mr McLeod cannot offer us another house until one comes free," he says. He is trying to be calm. He is thinking of himself and not of me. He knows they speak already in the town about his wife who is a shrew. He sees himself standing up tonight in front of all his friends in this Odd Fellow place and he sees himself an honourable member of this town. And then he hears my voice and what I say and is afraid I will embarrass him. Now, with all of this in his mind, he almost whispers what he says.

"Rosamund, we are here. And you will take your place among these people."

Then, before I can speak, he turns toward the stairs and goes. I hear him clomping down and through the hall and out the door. The dog barks. The rain falls. I am looking for my jar.

Thirteen dollars and forty-two cents. I am sitting on the floor. Thirteen dollars. I count it again. And forty-two cents. This is not enough. Not even half.

What am I going to do?

Maybe I could sell my things. To Proudfoot. Would she want to buy my plates? And papa's clock?

I crawl across the floor on my hands and knees and sit beside the trunk where it rests beneath the window. Just to turn the key and lift the lid takes all my will power. The smell of musty cleanliness is more than I can bear.

Now I am sitting here watching my things.

You will take your place among these people.

Someone downstairs opens the door. I am looking from the window. There is the moon. And there, in the yard, is the dog. It must be Alexandra's doing. Every night he goes out now to lift his leg against the fence. That much, at least, I have been able to teach these people.

The dog sits down. He looks along the street. And through the lighted windows of the house next door we listen to the gramophone. "There'll be a Hot Time in the Old Town Tonight!"

Suddenly the dog begins to howl. He throws back his head and sings. His voice goes yearning to the moon. My fingers dip and touch the surface of the plates. I lift my white-starched cap and place it on my head. I close my eyes. I listen to the dog. I cannot move. I howl.

March 1912

For two months, now, I do not bleed. But I will not tell Hans. I will save this news until I know for sure. Many women here miscarry. There is so much lifting to be done. Especially living on the upper floors. Up and down. Up and down. The ashes and the slops, the water and the wood. And winter. Sometimes I must bring in snow to melt for water. So I will save this news until I know. For sure.

April 1912

It is morning, and something is happening in the street.

"Hans, come here and look."

He is shaving. He comes up beside me, smelling of soap. We both look out the window.

Down below us the dogs are barking. People come running. Someone has brought a wagon with horses. Mrs Bailey is standing on her porch.

"What does it mean? Is their house on fire?"

Two of her sons come out, the youngest ones. They pull at her dress and weep.

"What is the matter?"

Hans does not answer.

Mr McLeod's automobile arrives. Mr Travis rides on the running board and he hops down into the snow.

"Hans? What is it?"

Hans does not answer. He wipes the soap from his face.

People are coming out from the Bailey's house. They carry furniture and put it on the wagon. Mrs Bailey screams at them to stop.

"What are they doing? *Hans*?"

He turns away. "They are being put out. Evicted. Bailey's drinking. Mr McLeod let him go."

I do not even speak. I throw on my coat and run down the stairs. Mrs Stuart is saying as I pass, "It serves them right. Them and that music. All that whisky when his kids are starving."

All I do is keep on running.

Half the street has gathered in the snow to watch. Barbarians. No one even goes to Mrs Bailey's side.

I find Mr McLeod and raise my arm to strike him.

Suddenly, Hans is behind me, pulling my arm and saying, "Don't! You mustn't! Do not interfere!"

All I know is I have threatened someone. And now I strike. At Hans. My tongue is freed. I speak. It is marvellous.

"Make this stop!" I am saying. "Make this stop!" To Mr McLeod. "Make this stop at once!"

Mr McLeod opens his mouth to speak, but I go on instead.

"You will not do this, Mr McLeod. It is monstrous and barbaric. I will not let you do it."

Mr McLeod looks at me. Surprised. No one has ever raised their hand to him before and I doubt that anyone has even raised their voice.

"Mrs Jensen –" he begins.

"Forgive me, Mr McLeod, but I will not, *cannot* let you do this. I am a Dane. I come from a civilized country. What you do to these people would not be permitted there. Courtesy would not permit it. Decency would not. The *law* would not."

He blinks. And slowly he begins to smile. It is a cold smile.

"Well, Mrs Jensen," he says. "You are quite the lady." He mocks me with his smile. "I shall do as you ask." Then he turns to Mr Travis. "Mr Travis! Have Mr Bailey's belongings taken back inside."

I am amazed.

"I thank you." That is all that I can say.

"You shouldn't thank me," Mr McLeod says. He is not smiling now. "That house" – and he points to the Baileys standing on their porch – "was to be *your* house. The one thing your husband told me that you wanted. Now," he shrugs, "you will have to wait for another." He turns and walks away.

I do not care. I do not care.

I have not bled for three months now. There is a life in me. And I have spoken with its voice.

I turn and look at Hans.

He is pale. He is alarmed. But he knows who I am.

I come inside and climb the stairs. I open the trunk. I take out papa's clock and set it on the table. I will even serve our breakfast on my plates.

Whatever else I know, I know now where I am. I am with me.

Rosamund Birghitta Jensen
died in Henley Point,
New Brunswick, at the age
of fifty-four in 1942.
She was the mother of
four boys and three girls.
The older ones speak Danish.

The Ukrainians

In the 1890's Canada opened its doors to immigration from Eastern Europe. The great Canadian prairies lay uncultivated, and farmers were needed to till the western soil.

Numerous wars had divided the people of Eastern Europe, and many lands were occupied by foreign powers. One such area was Ukraine, part of which was governed by Austria. There was considerable unemployment, and for many farmers land ownership was impossible. Dr Oleskiw, an agricultural expert, founded an organization to help the emigration of people of Galicia, as the area was then called. He wrote to the Canadian government, and subsequently toured western Canada and prepared a pamphlet for prospective emigrants. In 1895, ninety-four immigrants came to Canada and settled in Stuartburn, Manitoba. By 1900, Stuartburn had over three thousand immigrants from Ukraine, and numerous other Ukrainian settlements dotted the prairies.

At the same time, Poles, Austrians, Hungarians, and Czechoslovakians, Jews from all over Eastern Europe, and Germans also began to emigrate in significant numbers. They came in search of land, independence, religious freedom, and opportunity. The different waves of immigration reflected events in Europe: wars, depression, and crop failures, all brought people to Canada.

Immigration to Canada from Ukraine, for example, is usually divided into three waves of settlement: 1890 to 1919, 1920 to 1939, and the wave of immigration that followed the Second World War. It was difficult for all the newcomers, especially if they arrived just before winter without sufficient funds to see them through until they could find work in spring. However, they could often rely on relatives, and there was, in many cases, a sense of ethnic community and kinship. The most unfortunate were those who immigrated between 1926 and 1929. These immigrants had little time to put down roots before the years of Depression and drought.

In recent years the same strong feeling of the Ukrainian community has flowered into a sense of ethnic pride in the many accomplishments and successful endeavours of Ukrainians in Canada today.

1927

From Ukraine to a new life together on the Canadian Prairies

Old traditions brought from Ukraine married to the new land in the Canadian west joined the strengths of the old ways and the opportunities offered by the new. Though not always an easy union, it was strong and prospered.

The old ways would never be forgotten.
On the right days and occasions,
the ancient and long-living past was
still practised. To be Ukrainian is, among
so many other things, to remember as
well as to endure. Throughout the many
centuries of oppression there had
evolved distinctive customs like bread-
making, embroidery, and the wedding dance!

The fertile black earth of the homeland had been
cleared for hundreds of years. Here, everything was a
beginning. A tent would do for the good summer
weather, but something more substantial had to
follow soon. And throughout any weather, the work
was unceasing. This was a time for basic necessities.

There were no luxuries.

Nearly everything had to be done manually, and there could be no lazy or idle hands. Very little was ready-made. In the vast land each family had to be largely self-contained. Houses were often built from logs, and the interiors plastered with a simple mud mortar mixed and applied by hand.

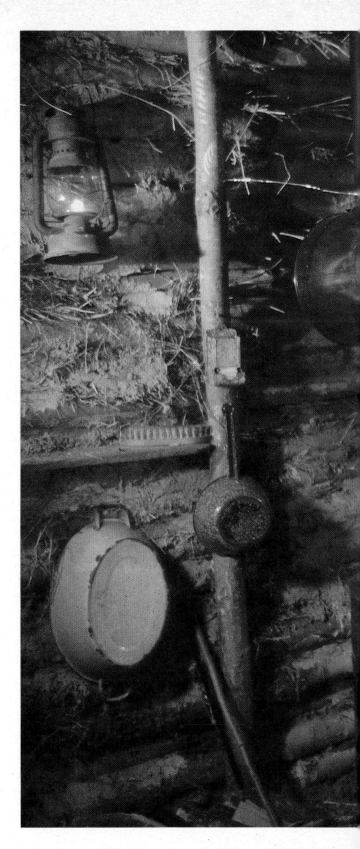

During the Depression, when farms could not produce enough to support families, many men left home to seek work for wages. Jobs were often to be found only after they had travelled great distances.

They had to take poorly paid, back-breaking jobs on the railways and in the mines. As hard as the labour was the loneliness of separation from their families, and the worries about their wives and children left alone on the homesteads.

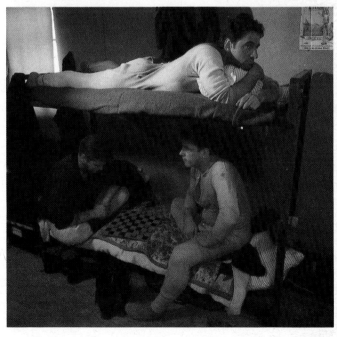

Former traditions
continued, but the
present could not
help but intrude.
Old icons, new icons:
pictures of the past
included those of the
recent past in the new
country. Traditions
flowed together.

Many of those who came to Canada and contributed so much to its growth and prosperity were destined to see the world of their youth fade, to grow old in a country not their own, to see the old ways change and their children move away, and to wait for the end with only memories and the ghosts of memories as company.

Visit from the Pension Lady

GEORGE RYGA

She came by today. In her little car that makes a tink, tink, tink *sound under the hood when she parks it in my front yard, near the lilac bush, and walks to where I'm standing.*

"Mr Lypa?"

"Yah."

"Mr Lypa –you've died," she tells me.

She has a briefcase in one hand, with "Government of Canada" printed on it. And I think to myself –the government of Canada comes to an old man's farm in a small Japanese car to tell him he's died! And thinking of that, I laugh to myself. If I was the government of Canada I would at least listen for a heartbeat before I pronounced a man dead.

The day I turned sixty-five started like any other day. There was a corner of garden to weed and the chicken coop to clean. The coop wasn't that messy, but the garden could use extra manure, particularly around the lilac shrub, which eats up manure and dead leaves like it had teeth just under the ground, chewing and digesting to beat hell. My son, Stefan, had sent me a box of chocolates. Why, I'll never understand. I still have my own teeth, but chocolate makes them ache now.

My sister Marina comes with her Dmitro just as I am pushing the first wheelbarrow of chicken manure across the garden.

"Bringing in the shit. We shall come rejoicing, bringing in the shit!" I sing loudly to the tune of a radio hymn.

Marina winces. Then, "Happy birthday, my brother," she says as she throws her arms around my neck. Then she shuts her eyes and brushes her cheek against mine. She steps back and with her eyes half shut she says, "May God give you many more years of good health."

For Marina God is like a strong light. She always squints or shuts her eyes when asking Him a favour or referring to Him as someone who's got more information than what's in the newspaper.

Dmitro stands behind her in his good suit, shoes all shined, pudgy hands opening and closing. He makes money, lots of money, from his clothing store. But she gives it away. And if you want to ask Dmitro an important question, you ask Marina. She answers for him, always has. But God must forgive me for such thoughts. These are good people. I owe them a lot. I will always owe them, for they raised my Stefan after Hanya died.

This young woman with the tink-tink *car and briefcase under her arm comes to tell me I've died. I look her over good, up and down.*

"How come they don't send a man to tell me?" I say to her. She don't like that. I can tell, but pretend I don't notice. "What's the matter – they afraid to send a man to talk to a man?"

The hurt shows in her soft, dark eyes.

Ivan, Ivan, I ask myself quietly, why do you do this? She is only doing what she is paid to do. You are old now with few rights and fewer needs, waiting for a pension to free you from worry.

"The damned pension hasn't come." The words are out, loudly, before I can stop them.

"I know. There have been problems."

"What problems? I'm sixty-five years old and I got no problems. Give me my pension!"

"I don't carry it in my pocket like a stick of chewing gum, sir. If I did, you'd have it."

I look her up and down again. I made a mistake about this one. She's not dumb. Not very respectful to an old man, either. She opens her briefcase and takes out a faded piece of newspaper, which she hands to me. My glasses are in the house, and even if I had them on my nose, I don't read English too good.

"What's it say?"

"It reports a mine cave-in in Timmins in 1934. You were listed as dead in the accident. You and a man named Olynyk," she tells me and puts the newspaper back in her briefcase.

Vladek . . . yes, Vladko Olynyk with the bad bones. He limped when he was tired after a shift underground. Something in his hips was wearing out. We went down the shaft together that morning. I stopped to tighten my shoelaces and he went ahead. I never saw him again.

I hear the groaning of the earth, the twisting and breaking of stone. Then the sulphuric smell, oddly sweet, of dust exploding from the shaft walls. I don't hear the roar of the cave-in ahead of me. There must've been one loud sound that did something to my ears. I don't hear too good for a week after. I know Vladek is dead. Nothing I can do about that. So I get the hell out of that mine. Down the road I go, out of Timmins, never turning back.

"They thought I was in there with Vladek?"

"Yes."

"I never punched out. Walked seventeen miles that day. Train came along and I went west, where you live longer."

She isn't listening. She looks past me, to the machine shed and empty barn. The barn Hanya built –with the other man. While I was away in the Crowsnest working for wages in a coal mine. Why does my heart still miss a beat and blood rush into my ears with the roar of a storm when I think of that? How old must a man get before he forgets jealousy?

"This farm. Did you homestead it?" the government woman asks me.

I sort of hear her and I don't.

I still remember Hanya, hunched in her worn mackinaw, big with child. Walking the tramped snow path from the house to the barn, from the barn to the haystack outside. Carrying forkfuls of timothy hay for the two milk cows. And behind her, two waterbuckets in his hands, the man whose name I didn't know. A fanatic light in his eyes, the mouth soft and fixed in a near-smile. He could've been an idiot, until you spoke to him.

"What the hell you doing in my house when I'm away?"

"I serve the Lord, brother. Your wife needed help."

I glare at Hanya. Help, indeed! I go away for a month and another man appears in my place. To help. Her belly showed before he came, so at least the child is mine.

I groan with doubt and guilt, an anger catches flame and burns inside of me, deafening me with harsh sounds, distorting my vision, confusing my sense of my own worth. I see them in the haystack, in my bed at night, like two frantic animals. She sees the thoughts devouring me and cries out in pain. The man is afraid. I approach him, my fists raised.

"Your wife needed help. She *asked* me to stay and help!" he whimpers, backing away from me.

"Leave my land at once!" I shout at him. She moans. I turn on her, my fists coming together over her head. She bows before me, ready for the blow. "Pack your things and go with him!"

"No!" she cries out, pleading. The man is hurrying away across the field towards the forest bordering the bank where the railway embankment cuts through the bottom edge of my farm. I point after him and yell, "Begone, whore!"

"Was this farm your homestead?"

The government lady with the baby car is asking me a question. I hear her but still don't understand.

"Hah?" My voice sounds like the bleat of a goat in my ears.

"If this farm is in your name, then that resolves whether you are alive or not!" She's smiling now. A pretty smile of someone who's not quite a woman,

but no longer a girl. I like her, but I'm not going to show it. Not me. Long ago I learned the best way to deal with government is to stare.

"No."

"No, what?"

"Farm's not in my name. When I took out the homestead, I put it in Hanya's name. The work I did, places I went to, I didn't know if I'd be dead or alive one day to the next. So everything's in her name."

"Why?"

"To be a widow's bad enough. To have nothing is worse than death."

How little a young man knows of how the world will grind and twist him. Thrown this way and that by fear, hunger, cold, and helplessness, what time was there for tenderness and sorrow? So when I have no answers, I stare.

I learned to stare on board the Gdynia, the floating Polish tub that brought me to Canada. I never had vermin on my body and I was not Polish. But I was deloused and had my head shaved, and the passport I carried was the passport of Poland. I had to have a health certificate before I could leave for Canada. The village doctor, drunk and stinking of vomit, told me I had an ear infection. His open, trembling hand moved across the clinic table to stop in front of me, palm up, when he told me this. I put five zlotys into it. In that moment the ear infection cleared. Twenty zlotys would've cured a cancer. He stamped my passbook with good health as I stared.

"To be an immigrant widow in Canada then was like walking blind among snakes."

She laughs at that. The laugh of an honest woman – the laugh Hanya had when I first met her.

"What's your name?"

"Nancy. Nancy Dean," she says.

And just like that, I know! She isn't Anglo-Saxon, not with that face. Yet, I'm not sure she is one of us.

"What's your real name?"

She says nothing. From the corner of my eye, I see her bite her lip, the colour rise in her cheeks. She throws her head back, like a nervous mare. Oh, my child, if I was young again we would

*have better things to do than talk about old men
who've lost their names.*

*But I was young once. How much dancing and
playing did I do then?*

*This homestead is where all the youth was
drained out of me. On this homestead with a two-
bladed axe, then out on the road seeding and
harvesting other men's lands from Manitoba to the
western mountains, cutting pulpwood, mining,
railroading. Surviving a depression. The next
generation might dance. But for Hanya, Dmitro,
Marina, and me, youth ended before it started. We
danced at our weddings. Then we worked.*

"*What's your name? Your real name?*" *I ask her
again.*

"*What difference would it make, Mr Lypa?*"

"*In my heart I know this – there was no people
named Dean in Halychina,*" *I say to her. I could
say more, but I want to hear it from her.*

"*My grandfather's name was Odinsky. He was a
Russian Jew.*"

"*When he landed in Halifax, Odinsky was hard
to spell, so they gave him the name Dean!*" *I
gloat, slapping my knee.*

"*Yes.*" *She looks at me nervously.*

*Child, I know what you are thinking – a flood
of despair passes like a winter chill through my
body. I will not deny the pogroms as you must not
deny the poverty that brought us both to this
country and this place. Here we both stand on an
old man's farm, two branches of the same body,
and still we tremble in each other's presence.*

"*I knew your grandfather,*" *I tell her.* "*He was a
good man.*"

She is surprised. "*He never spoke of you. Where
did you meet him?*"

"*Everywhere. He was the city man, the rag-
and-bone man, the shoe merchant. I was a country man. We spoke the same language. We needed
each other to explain what we couldn't understand by ourselves. I knew him.*"

*I say it the best way I know how. Maybe she
understands, maybe not. My Stefan is a bachelor,
but if he was married and had a son, could I explain to my grandson how I ordered his grandmother from her house, banishing her after a*

*man who would die that night? And how she
begged to stay, her spirit and health broken?*

The other man died. Just below this farm, on the
railway track. When I ordered him away, he blun-
dered through the snow, staggering from side to
side like a drunkard.

"Go with him!" I had shouted.

"No, Ivan! Please! I am not guilty of what you
think!" Her outcry of innocence still haunts my
dreams with guilt even today.

He had carried a cross to my house, I was told.
The same cross he carried to the doorsteps of
other homesteaders. Looking for converts to
some god he created in his sad mind, for the poor
devil couldn't read or write. He walked away
across my field, sliding through deep snow down
to the railway. A wind began blowing suddenly,
covering fields and forests in a white mass of
snow cloud. He walked the track in this blizzard
until the train came. Maybe he was blinded and
ran towards the train, and death. This I know –
the train hit him and threw him aside. He was
found a week later when the section gang came
by and saw one of his legs sticking out of the
snow.

*She stands before me, unsure of herself. Not sure of
how to take me, which is the way I prefer it until
she tells me she's a friend. Not just somebody working for the government. She opens her briefcase
again and takes out a notebook and a pen.*

"*What you say is interesting, Mr Lypa. But it
doesn't help. Perhaps you have some surviving
friends.*"

*Hell, it's like a game of checkers I played during
winter nights in the section-gang bunkhouses. I
make a move, she makes a move. But this is not a*

bunkhouse and she is not a workmate. The game bores and angers me.

"How much do you earn a month?" I ask. She blinks but doesn't answer.

"I'm sixty-five years old. I got a right to a pension. That's all I got to say. If you don't understand, turn your car around and get out of here! Tell your government to go to hell, too!" I'm shouting at her and my pulse is racing.

I turn away from her and walk into my house, shutting the door hard behind me. I wait to hear the sound of her car starting and driving away. I wait and wait.

I call him *mazur*, my friend. He is Polish, and to me every Pole is a *mazur*. For the bishop of Warzawa he would have given his right arm. As he would have for the Polish gentry, who exported him as so much meat to dig tunnels and lay railway track.

"Wake up, *mazur*!" I shake him in the morning. "The Bolsheviks have taken Warzawa and they've started making babies inside your sister and mother!"

He sits up and crosses himself with a hand that's as large as a line-man's shovel. Then he clears his throat and spits behind his bed.

"You blaspheme all you want, *hutzul*. One day you'll pay for it."

"How? I have no money."

"Something will go wrong with your back. I've seen it happen to other men with no respect for God or homeland," he says sadly. I laugh. He is funniest when he is most serious.

"When that happens I go straight to a doctor," I say.

"Won't do any good. When it happens you're a cripple the rest of your life. There's no doctor alive who can heal the judgement of God, *hutzul*."

We work together, argue, make soup for each other. At night we play cards or checkers and talk of our families. Born a Pole, he never learned to read or write his language. I read his letters from his mother, and write replies to them as if she was my own mother. When Hanya and I marry he works his and my shift for three days. When I offer to return the money he earned for me he won't take it.

"Maybe one day I'll marry and go away for three days. Then you can do the same for me," he says.

"How could that be? Who'd marry a *mazur*?" I reply, but I don't mean that.

We part on a warm spring morning after a trainload of immigrants had been dropped off at the station where we both worked. They are frightened, tired people. Children holding on to their sleeves, their possessions in woven trunks and cloth bags piled high on the platform. We nod to young women, older than their time, their heads covered in tied kerchiefs. They smile as we approach, while the men stare into the wind, looking angry.

The *mazur* and I know what they are thinking. How scared they are of failure, starvation, degradation.

"Welcome to Canada." The words come out of both our throats at the same moment, in the two languages they all understand. There is sudden laughter, chatter about their long voyage, questions about where to wash their children and prepare food. We take them to our bunkhouse.

The *mazur* motions to me and we step outside. The sound of the immigrants coming to life inside the small building is like music to me. My heart is bursting with joy. I wish for Hanya to be here with me instead of on the cold, lonely homestead where she is plastering walls and milking cows.

"I'm leaving for northern Ontario. The foreman said yesterday the railway is transferring men," he tells me.

I hear a child cry inside the bunkhouse.

"Good. I'll go with you. I've had enough of the bald, windy places. Maybe Ontario is better and I can bring Hanya out to start life all over," I tell him, excitement building in me so much I have to open the buttons on my tunic to cool off. The *mazur* turns away from me, shaking his head.

"You don't understand," he says. "Only I am going. The foreman said they only want one man."

Again my heart races. With regret, sorrow. I cannot see myself working alone without this *mazur*. This flat-faced fool in cracked boots who crosses himself before he eats, his fingers bleeding with broken calluses as he thanks God for the watery turnip soup we are about to swallow. Who gives some of his earnings each month to the church, and sends some to his mother in Warzawa. Who does without tobacco or a new shirt so others close to his memory will not forget him. He walks away, his shoulders hunched, his legs stumbling under his body.

"Hey, *mazur*!" I shout after him, fighting back my tears.

He turns. "*Mazur*, write to me sometimes. Tell me where you are and what you are doing!"

"Don't make fun of me now. You know I can't write." There are tears in his eyes and his voice is hoarse. I wave him on and go into the bunkhouse to join the immigrants.

Mazur, mazur – how did you live? And where are you now? In some old men's home, or under the earth? You are on my mind, as is she, the wife I lost so quickly. The mother of my Stefan, of whom I was not worthy. Had the *mazur* and I remained in the old country, we would have been enemies, maybe soldiers in two different armies. We might have shot each other to death for the honour of homelands that had no use for us. Yet thrown upon each other as we were for a few short seasons in this country, we became closer than brothers, more loving than we were to our wives, sisters, and children.

The door opens and she stands over me.

"*I asked you to go away. Get in your goddamned car and never come back.*"

"*Later. But first, may I make us both some coffee?*"

"*Sure . . . sure.*"

I'm too tired to be angry with her any more. She drops the briefcase on the table and busies herself heating water on the propane stove.

"*Your landing card, immigration documents, something must be available.*"

"My Canadian papers got burned. Hanya was burning old catalogues and letters long ago. She made a mistake."

"*But you've applied for a re-issue, have you not?*"

How difficult to make a child understand. "Yes, I applied. But they sent me all kinds of questions – a big envelope of questions I didn't know how to answer."

"*All we have to establish is one date – one recorded date on which you were alive after your presumed death in that mine. Something more than your word.*"

"What's the matter with my word? I've bought seventeen cows, eight horses, and all my farm equipment on my word and a handshake!" *I roar at her now.*

"*We are not trading horses here! I cannot prepare a statement from such information.*" *She's mad too. I can see it by the way her cheeks have gone white and her mouth tight as she looks at me while she's making coffee.*

For a long while we don't speak. The water hisses on the stove, then bubbles. She removes it and pours it over coffee grounds in the pot. She brings coffee mugs and the pot to the table and sits across from me, her hands under her chin. I look at her, so small at this big table, and laugh. She laughs with me.

"*When you were first married, what was it like?*"

"Shame on you – go try it for yourself!" *I say to her and she blushes.*

"*I didn't mean . . . that. How difficult was it to live?*"

"Ay. It was difficult. Everything is difficult. It is difficult not to have an education. I often think if I had been born to a different mother I might've been a doctor or a train conductor. It's difficult to live longer and see more than my own father did. When I was born, men scythed fields and women flailed grain on the threshing floor. Here in Can-

ada, I guided a walking plough pulled by two horses. Today, twice a day, I see a jet airplane fly over my farm carrying people who never see me, I'm that small." I try to explain everything I know in as few words as possible, but it takes a long time to say it right. The effort leaves me out of breath.

"I don't understand what you're saying."

What can I expect from someone this young? I try again.

"It's too fast. I should live two hundred years to see everything I've been and lived through. And what have I learned? From one hurry-up day to another, a short summer followed by a long winter, then another and another. Even this comes as it comes to a blind man. I was bent to the ground, tearing out tree roots and stones to make food. Cutting trees waist deep in snow. Repairing track to keep trains running in a straight line."

"You are a religious man, then?"

"No – never!" That stung me. *"I've been called many things in my time. But never a religious man. For women, that's something else. I suppose my Hanya did some praying when I wasn't around. I came to Canada so I wouldn't ever bend my knee to another man. For me, the road to God was barred by the priest. When I was a small boy, I say to myself – if I'm that important to God, if I'm really someone he worries about, then he must show me another road. Once I stood in a meadow, and I yelled to the clouds, 'Show me! I demand you show me another way than churches with fat, sleepy priests in the pay of police and feudal landlords!'*

"I waited until night for an answer. I lay on the grass, exhausted. The sky got dark, but there was silence. Either God had no answer, or there was no room in his temple for a man like me. I walked home in the dark to my father's cottage, thinking if God has no time or answers for me, fine. I'll find freedom in my own way."

"Did you?" Again she asks the questions that are so hard to answer.

"No. There is no freedom for the living." I am tired of talking. There is a pain in my head. She

eats information without chewing. If I gave her my whole life on a platter she would eat it in ten swallows and bang with her spoon on the plate for more.

I came to visit my son at Marina and Dmitro's house. I came loaded with gifts, for he was a boy and what little I had sent to support him was not enough. Not in money. Somehow I always found money. It was not being there except on holidays, and always in their house, with all its decorations of the Ukraine. Embroidered cloth under and over anything that cost more than fifty dollars to buy. The Ukrainian calendars, printed in New York, with the saints' days in red, paper flowers in vases, and the plaster crucifix of a tormented Christ with a face of a dim-witted store clerk I once knew hanging there night and day.

I laugh with sorrow when I come into their house. Sometimes I have to have a few drinks before I find the courage to come through their door. After the first roar of laughter, I have to be quiet. They all learned to speak softly, so softly I put my hand to my ear and call, "Eh? What'd you say?"

Dmitro, the merchant, is now wearing a small English moustache. A white shirt and dark tie. His shoulders hunch – not with the weight of the world's cares, but with humiliation at his own civility. He joins every club that will have him, but he is restless and pushed by things he does not speak about.

My sister, thin and withdrawn, polishes and cleans as if the stains of terrible sin were coated on all she owns. A leader of the local branch of the nationalist language organization, consumed with hatred and distrust of her homeland, now a socialist state for almost as long as she has lived. She is at the sink, cleaning. I come up behind her and put my hands on her shoulders. She becomes rigid, like an icicle.

"Let Dmitro and me do that," I say, laughing.

She shrugs. "This is not a man's work."

"In the old country, the communists made a law that says men and women who work in factories should cook and wash dishes together when they come home."

She drops the cloth in the sink and stares out the window. I watch the reflection of her eyes in the glass.

"Godlessness is no joke, Ivan. Neither is the slavery of our people."

I press my cheek against the tight curls of her hair. They smell rubbery and seared. She draws away. I sit at the table again and sigh.

"What's wrong, Ivan? Have I upset you?"

"Ask your husband. He may still remember the words spoken by dying men. I came to see my son. And to taste dark bread, which has vanished from my world."

Dmitro coughs and pulls a chair back to sit across from me.

"Shall we talk about the old days?" he asks.

"The boy is asleep. I will wake him soon," my sister explains, wiping her hands on her apron. "I've enrolled Stefan in language school this past winter."

I am delighted. And just as quickly a chill goes down my back. For I had not been asked – I am told for the first time. Why such a decision without my thoughts?

"I . . . I'm glad," I say, faking cheerfulness. "Is he going to be able to read the old poetry and stories in the old books?"

Marina looks to Dmitro for a reply, and Dmitro looks down at his hands.

"I don't know. We both had some schooling in the old country, but such books were forbidden to us, if they existed. I think if Stefan can learn to read and write and speak the language, that is enough."

I am on my feet at once, pointing at both of them, ashamed of my anger but helpless to control it. "I don't want my son crippled by ignorance the way we were! To learn a dialect of a language – which is all we learned – is not enough! He must have the best. If it's money he needs,

some way I'll move heaven and earth to pay. But he must have nothing less!"

Now she's angry, shaking her small fist at me. "Ah! Listen to this father, setting the world to rights again! Look at him – homeless, calloused – a *muzhik* with nothing but a useless homestead to his name – demanding that his son become nothing less than a *hetman*! Who do you think you are to come here roaring like some wild animal?"

She's right. I sit down and bury my head in my arms. My ignorance and my pride are my own undoing. Too long I've neglected what is dearest to me, and now I again threaten the welfare of my own child.

"What sort of school have you put him in to learn the language?" I ask. I already know the answer.

"The church runs language classes. I take him there and help the priest by keeping the children under control," she tells me quietly.

I feel a touch on my shoulder and raise my head. Stefan is standing beside my chair, sleepy-eyed, smiling. My heart swells inside me. I embrace him and lift him to the ceiling.

"Look at what I brought you!" I say to him. Together we open the parcels. A shawl for Marina, a bottle for Dmitro. And at the bottom of the last parcel, a train carved of wood for Stefan.

"Push it, pull it. Do anything you wish with it. Nothing will break even if you throw it!" I demonstrate as I explain by running the train and cars around the table. "Who knows, one day you may be a train engineer with your old man working on the section to keep your train running on schedule through all kinds of weather."

He smiles and takes the train from me to push on the tabletop by himself.

"That's it, Stefan, that's it! As soon's you grow up, I'll talk to my section foreman about getting you on with me. We'll make a team. They'll put our names in a book for what we did!"

My days on the railway have ended when we finally work together, taking hay off this field. He is a good worker with a strong body. But his lungs are weak, like his mother's. In the dust he coughs and sweats. I take the hard work myself. In the evening we walk across the field on our way to the house. He is seventeen now, and a soft, silky beard is making its first appearance on his cheeks. We walk side by side.

"Do you like it here, Stefan?" I ask him.

"It's hard to make a living, but I feel good."

"It's hard to make a living, that's true. But the air in the mornings is so pure. The soil has stones, but with good cultivation crops will always grow. There will be enough to eat for the two of us."

"You need more land, father." Stefan walks slower now, his face troubled.

"No problem. We can clear another twenty acres of bush. Right after harvest we can start. Cut up and sell the bigger trees for firewood. Next spring, we break the ground and every bit of land that can be used on this homestead will be planted." I am so excited just thinking of my son working alongside of me. But he shakes his head, looking away from me. We stop in the field, and I turn him to face me.

"That's not what I want, father."

"In the house I'll build an extra room for you so you've got your own place to sleep. It won't be as fancy as your uncle's place, but it will be clean with lots of windows for the sun." I try to keep my voice from sounding like I'm begging. For I am begging, my eyes filling with tears, my hands beginning to shake.

"I'll come and help you in the summers. But I can't live with you."

"Why not? Are you ashamed of me because of who I am? That I never had a house in the city, or a new car? This isn't a mud hut I'm living in, you know!" Stop it, my heart is pleading with my brain. The boy is in pain and your words cut him as sharply as if they were knife blades. But I cannot stop. All that should be said gently and in good time now comes in a torrent that I cannot contain.

"I did not give you up. I would, if I could, have cared for you myself. But who would hire a man in the mines or on the wheatlands when he came with a child? What life would that have been for

you? Soon after you were born, I carried your mother in my arms down that road, hoping for a truck or wagon to come along and get her to the hospital. For two hours I carried her before help came. I was going out of my mind, so was she, because we had to leave you behind in your crib. I ran all the way back to tend to you. I forgot to even say goodbye to her, and she never came back alive. Now you are a man. I like your uncle and aunt – I love them, but I do not admire them. They are timid, and they settle for little. I would have wished for stronger people to raise you."

His eyes flash with indignation. I've erred in criticizing them, but it had to be said. He is my son, and I must be honest with him.

"They are good people!" His voice is thin and accusing.

"If that were enough I would apologize to them and you. For me, poor as I am, that is not enough. They are settling for a tray of coloured eggs at Easter and promises they will never taste! Nothing is ever given to those who wait quietly. The Depression divided you from me. It killed your mother. I know men who say we must organize and fight to become real citizens. And I know others who want nothing to do with that. Which answer is the right one?"

He shakes his head wildly, backing away from me. "I don't know what you are saying. I've never heard such talk before!"

I reach out to him, embrace him in my arms, stroke his head to comfort him. How sweet and helpless he is! How obstinate. I hear his heart pound against mine, rapidly, like that of a bird.

"The truth is the truth. We can do nothing about that. Child, I speak in fear when I speak this way. I want you to move away from the shadow of a priest's skirts. This country has no time for such customs. A father's love, a folk song – that is for women and old men now. If we get to be known for that only, we're lost." I speak softly to him. He sobs and shudders, but remains pressed against me.

"I'm sorry, but I must go to church. I am a Christian and always will be, father." Saying this, he kisses me and withdraws from my embrace.

"Yes, I understand." I am dry inside, my mouth tasting of dust. For the first time in my life I am conscious of aging with each heartbeat in my chest. Staring into a cold wind that somehow moves past me like the passing of my life. Stefan wipes his eyes on his shirt sleeve.

"I don't want to farm, father. I'll help you but I can't come here to live. I want to finish school and go to university. Train to become a school teacher," he says, his eyes pleading with me for approval.

There was once a teacher in my family. Uncle Mikita, who lived two doors down the street in our village. He was a tall, stooped man with the sharp, clear eyes of an eagle. When his brow knit with anger, heaven darkened.

"Don't read Shevchenko like nuns murmuring prayers at sunset. Read him with fists clenched, blood racing in your ears, your eyes turned to the uplands of the spirit!" he would shout at his classes while they quivered, their eyes averted in terror. For in the streets and in their homes they were now cringing before occupation troops and government agents of yet another foreign state.

One evening, my uncle was returning from the library. Two drunken soldiers staggered out of the tavern dragging behind them their bayoneted rifles, which clattered on the cobbles. They saw my uncle approach. One winked at the other and raised his rifle. My uncle came abreast of them and the soldier stabbed at the books my uncle carried. The bayonet pierced the cover of the outer book, knocking it to the street.

"Stop!" the soldier slurred in a Polish dialect. "Are you a horse or a goat? Identify yourself!"

Both soldiers laughed. My uncle watched them silently, his eyes burning with contempt and fury. He bent down to pick up his damaged book.

"Ah, Yantik, he is a dog – a field dog. Notice how he falls on all fours. Bark for us, dog!" the soldier ordered. Slowly, my uncle's hand reached for a loose cobble. But the other soldier saw the move and brought the butt of his rifle down on my uncle's hand, smashing it with a crunching noise. My uncle still made no sound, but blood trickled from his lips as he chewed on his tongue with pain.

"I said bark for us!" the first soldier squealed in panic, for a crowd was quickly gathering along the street. My uncle looked up at him.

"You wretched fool," he said softly. His last words. For with a sudden motion, the soldier pulled his rifle back and lunged at my uncle, burying the bayonet to the hilt in his back. My uncle coughed and slowly, his head drooping first, died on the street where he taught children to read the poetry of Taras Shevchenko with pride.

Late afternoon. The hum of flies is a sleepy sound in the warm kitchen. We sit facing each other, like a father and daughter.

"My grandfather is like you," she tells me. "You should visit him at the retirement home sometimes."

"Why?" I ask.

"He is opinionated, argumentative." She begins to laugh. And I laugh with her. I laugh because she thinks I need another old man to argue my remaining days with.

"He is also certain he'll never die, and convinced he never lived," she continues.

"Enough!" I say to her. "Enough. Give me his address. I may see him, I may not. Depends on my mood. But not because you asked!"

It is like talking to a fence post. I stop laughing, but she seems to find that even more amusing. I clamp my jaws together tight and stare. She pours me another coffee – even sugars and stirs it for me, as if I was some thirsty paralytic. I have let her stay too long. Now it will be difficult to get her to leave. But she stops laughing and reaches for her papers again.

"No bank records, social insurance number? Nothing since the mine accident?"

I grunt.

"What about hospitalization?"

"Never been sick."

"There's always a statutory declaration you can sign after I've prepared it, supported by the declarations from your sister and brother-in-law, as well as your son."

"Never! I would rather die than have my family swear I am alive and needing money! You think I have no pride?"

Now she understands. She is nodding and thinking as she watches me.

"That only leaves criminal convictions. Have you ever been arrested and convicted of a crime?"

I'm not replying. I don't want to talk about it – not to her, not to anybody. No pension is worth that. I would rather starve, beg, steal. But I'm not talking about it! She looks at me for a long moment, suspecting. Then her eyebrows raise and a smile forms on her lips. Not a friendly smile. A pension-lady smile.

"It's your pension. And my responsibility for seeing you get it, Mr Lypa."

"Go to hell!"

She pushes the paper away and taps the table with her pen. Like a hen pecking on a tin pail. She is still thinking. For a long time she is thinking before she speaks.

"If I have to, I'll talk to your sister and her husband, or your son."

"You keep Stefan out of this, you hear? He's a busy man, principal of a school and not to be bothered!" I try to keep control of myself, but my words are tripping over each other, I'm that mad.

"Then you tell me!"

Jesus, her eyes are like steel. Whoever trained her trained a policeman. Now I don't like her, but I'm a little bit scared of her, too.

"All I'm after is a recorded date of conviction that is later than the mine accident in which you were listed dead. Give that to me and where it happened and you've got your pension."

"You'll never find out."

"Don't worry. I'll find out."

Three years after Vladek died, I was in Vancouver. I'm walking past the post office. There is a big meeting on the street. Unemployed workers holding a meeting to demand jobs. I've given money to the labour temple, but I never went on a demonstration because I've been around the country enough to think you can't squeeze water from a stone. There's nothing to do and no meeting will change that, I'm thinking. But I stop to listen.

There're angry people listening to the speaker. And the speaker's angry. Even the pavement of the street feels hot and mad. I don't see the police – nobody does. They attack from behind where I stand. Clubbing this way and that, grabbing men and pulling them away. Two of them knock me to the ground. Well, I'm a pretty big man in those days. I kick one in the chin and throw the other one as far as the building wall. Then I'm on my feet and running.

"Get that sonofabitch!" I hear one of the policemen yell. I'm in an alley when they grab me the second time. I fall down and they've got me by the pantlegs. I get to my hands and knees and try to tear away from them. But my suspenders break and I'm out of my pants.

They take me in my shirt and underwear to the police station. They say they are going to charge me with unlawful assembly and resisting arrest. But when I come to court next morning a judge with a moustache that completely covers his mouth, asks me if I was guilty of something called indecent exposure.

"Sure," I say, looking at that moustache and grinning, because I wonder how the sound came out so clear from his mouth with so much hair covering the hole.

He sentences me to seven days in jail, but I never see what the jail is like, because after sentence I am taken to the room where there are a lot of men – some from the demonstration meeting, others drunks, thieves, murderers. When they divide us up after the morning court, I get mixed up with someone else and I walk out the door with the innocent ones and nobody calls me back or tries to stop me.

Outside the kitchen window, my field seems on fire in a red glow from the setting sun. I feel stiff and drained. We have both drunk some brandy from a bottle I had saved for Christmas. She has been writing for an hour now. Meadowlarks are singing, but she does not hear them as she writes. I feel like a dead man, sitting in a wooden chair, waiting for the last forms to be filled before they lower me into the earth.

If I was the government, I would listen for a heartbeat first . . . .

The Italians

It is little more than a fluke of history that Italy did not lay claim to all of the western hemisphere and that today our major language is not Italian, since the stunning discoveries of the fifteenth century were made by Italian explorers. Their voyages were, however, sponsored by other countries, as Italy was not unified at the critical period of exploration and colonization, but remained a collection of city-states and small kingdoms well into the nineteenth century. Thus, its sea-going expertise benefited other countries: Columbus sailed under the Spanish flag; Caboto –John Cabot – claimed land for England; Giovanni da Verrazano explored for France.

The first Italian immigrants who came to Canada were from the aristocracies of the city-states. The Crisafi brothers who came in 1674 from Messina, Sicily, became commanders of a post at Niagara, then part of New France. Over the years a trickle of immigration from the city-states in northern Italy continued, often by way of France or England.

After the unification of Italy in 1870, the emigration pattern altered, largely as a result of changed economic conditions in the country. Northern Italy became industrialized, and as its economy improved, the economy of southern Italy deteriorated. Poor wages from wealthy landowners, few educational opportunities, and poverty were the conditions of existence for many in the south.

Canada was a place for a new beginning, and the hard-working, forward-looking people of southern Italy began to migrate. Some came at the turn of the century to work on the railroad, and they were followed by their families and their family's friends.

Southern Italy was dominated by the extended family system. Emigration often meant leaving one's family or being separated from them for many years until money was saved to provide for them. Once they arrived in Canada, all members of the family worked, and money was pooled for mutual assistance. Very often the goal was to purchase a small business, since being in business was the measure of success.

The Depression and the Second World War stopped Italian immigration for a time. The war devastated the Italian economy, and southern Italy continued to fall behind as the industrial north rebuilt. After the war, however, more Italians than ever emigrated.

Most came because they wanted to work, and because they had a brother, a sister, or a cousin in Canada. Poor and overpopulated southern Italy offered no future for the ambitious and for those who longed to see their children educated and successful. Sometimes the longing for the homeland continued –a longing for family ties, and for the rolling hills and memories of the sea. The "homeland" was often romanticized after long years of absence; poverty was often forgotten in face of adjustment and success in the new land.

1978

Italia mia. My Italy. My home.

The land, loved so passionately and tended so carefully, could no longer nourish her people

Here in the south, families had lived and farmed for centuries. For a man to own his own *terreni,* his own land, was a source of pride and honour. But the land was worn out, and it had been divided again and again among brothers for generations. So they set out from Calabria, from Puglia, from Abruzzi, to find work and opportunity in a new land.

Some of the men brought their families with them; but many had to go alone, hoping to be reunited later. They were used to a life of hard work, so the physical demands of the new world could be met; but the loneliness was painful for a closely knit people. The strangeness of the language and culture, of the very environment of everyday life, encouraged them to save money: some would be sent home to help those left behind or to be put away penny by penny to pay for their passage. Once enough money had been saved, wives and children joined their men, and together they began to work for their future in a new country with new customs and manners. Not all was left behind, however. Many traditional values thrived as the family grew.

Prosperity brought change, but much remained the same

Family-run businesses were built with love and long hours of hard work. As in the old country, all members of the family took part in the enterprise. As they flourished, their influence on their new society was felt more and more strongly.

The cultures flowed together.
Just as Canadian Italians were changed
by this country, so their past has become
a part of what we are in the present.

Guido

DAVID C. HUMPHREYS

It began in the church. On entering, Guido slid into a pew and bowed his head reverently. The light above the altar gleamed through the thick, red glass. God was in His Church. But when Guido lifted his head, there, beneath the visible presence of God, lounged the young priest who would be performing the marriage. Not only lounging but wearing an old windbreaker and sneakers.

The priest clapped his hands like a football coach and ordered him, Guido Vitelli, to stand at the front with his daughter, Angela. And there he stood while the priest rummed and tummed some jazz tune for the bridegroom to fox-trot down the aisle to. Guido was mortified.

He glanced sidelong at his daughter, so dark, so vital, so like a young Italian girl should be. Angela! And he squinted at the groom, a tall, blond Anglo dressed in jeans, and he wondered why he himself had worn a suit. Young Bainbridge stood there at ease, armoured in the indifference of one born to this country. Guido sweated in his suit as he realized this was the way it would be during the actual ceremony, too. Guido Vitelli, squat and swarthy, a clown on public view. The rehearsal was but the prelude. Yes, that was where it had begun.

His discomfiture continued at the little reception given at his house after the rehearsal. The whole Vitelli family was there and so was the groom's mother and father. Bainbridge, what a good and proper name that was! How solid and firm on the Canadian earth! All his immigrant life in Canada, Guido had felt the presence of one Bainbridge or another. And now he was compounding servility with stereotype. He went to find Scotch for Mr Bainbridge and poured a breakfast glass full for himself. He knew he was acting larger than life, performing to their view of the operatic Italian, but he could not help himself. His eldest son, Filippo, unwittingly abetted the image, for Filippo was sweating profusely and wiping himself mechanically with a large handkerchief printed in an outrageous, florid design. And Constanze, Filippo's wife, billowed over half the couch and was constantly wiping one child's nose or adjusting the bow on a frilly dress for another.

Guido sank within himself. The noise level rose as the children ran shrieking, deliciously out of hand. Franco, his wise, middle son, stood like an aloof rock amidst the eddying children. No gleam of sweat marred the classic lines of his olive face. No child laid a sticky hand on his superbly cut suit. He was a forbidding figure, and yet, that was simply another image for the Bainbridges, Guido thought. He knew what kind of Italian they imagined his lawyer-son to be.

"Nonno! Nonno!" chanted the children. "Be a bear! Chase us!"

But Guido brushed them aside, though normally he would have been delighted to don the ragged old fur rug and play the grizzly. Instead he rushed to Mr Bainbridge, the bottle of Scotch thrust forward.

"More Scotch, Mr Bainbridge!"

"I'm just fine, Mr Vitelli."

"Guido! Call me Guido! I told you before!"

"Guido."

"What an excellent drink, this Scotch! But, could it be too old?"

"No," said Mr Bainbridge, an odd look on his face. "Not too old."

"Really," said Guido. "When I make my own wine, I always drink it young."

Mr Bainbridge excused himself but the ice clinked in his glass as his hand shook. Mrs Bainbridge came over, a small fox-faced woman, trailing a perfume that was severe and expensive all at the same time. Lavender, thought Guido, remembering the scents of his youth and English old maids who always wore it on the tours. He bowed to her.

"We should be going home, Ted," she said. Mr Bainbridge stood, checked.

Guido spread his arms. "Stay! Stay as long as you like!"

"Oh, no. We've presumed on your wonderful hospitality long enough."

"Wonderful," echoed her husband.

Guido bowed his head and looked at her archly. "In a week's time, dear Mrs Bainbridge, I shall give my little girl to the wonderful boy, your son." And he took her hand and kissed it, breathing across the hard knuckles like a beach gigolo. There, he thought, now I have committed the final indignity.

The cash register rang in accompaniment to the tinkle of tiny hammers inside Guido's head. He smiled bravely at the customer and deftly wrapped her purchases. Filippo was happily banging large cans of whole tomatoes one atop the other, his face wrinkled with concentration. Two more and he'll bring the whole pile down again, thought Guido.

"Filippo! Look outside for your mother," Guido ordered.

"You can see her coming," said Filippo, the final can poised in his hand.

Guido grinned suddenly. Antonia certainly favoured bright colours, rejecting the eternal black that was once the dress of married women. Anyway, she was still a fine figure of a woman, brightness became her.

"Look anyway."

Filippo put the can back in the case. Guido sighed with relief. The pyramid of cans would remain upright. He frowned. He had staggered into bed last night and his dreams had been bad ones. Had he woken Antonia? Was that why she was late?

Another customer came up to the cash register and Guido served her. As he punched in the figures, his hand touched the envelope by the cash drawer. He did not open it. The clear rectangle where his name and address showed had told him all he needed to know.

Filippo came back inside.

"She's coming. Mrs Shapiro stopped to talk to her."

A car drew up outside, a long car, sleek with a heavy chrome grille.

"Franco. That's his car," said Guido, nodded amiably to the customer. Filippo did not look surprised. He must have known Franco was coming.

"Stay here, Filippo. Look after the front."

Guido tucked the envelope into his coat pocket and strode to the storeroom at the back of the shop. He glanced around and then found a box of lettuce. He picked it up and carried it dripping to the galvanized-zinc counter. The heads of lettuce rolled in disorder before him.

He heard the door swing open.

"Papa," said Franco. Antonia was with him. He turned and took out the envelope. Quietly and deliberately, he tore it into shreds and threw them into the puddles of water that dripped from the lettuce. Franco looked at him with sad and knowing eyes.

"That won't make it go away, papa," he said. "You have thirty days. Mr Tomassino didn't think you were being reasonable or you'd have had ninety."

Guido stripped a lettuce of its outer leaves. The tearing of the envelope had been the extent of his anger. Now he was thinking.

"He offered you a deal?"

"The plaza," said Antonia. "He wants you to have a store in the plaza."

"Take it," said Franco. "Go see him. He could be generous."

Guido bagged the lettuce and picked up another. Tomassino, that one-time barber. How quietly he had bought property on the block. Guido had to admire that, but he wouldn't give in.

"That's not a new deal. My answer's still no."

"Papa, thirty days from now, this store won't be standing and you'll have no deal."

"What deal is a plaza ten miles away? Will he pay the bus fare for my customers to get up there?"

"You'll have new customers," said Antonia. "Man as good as you, there'll be plenty of customers — and no deadbeats either."

"I'm sixty years old," Guido said, and at that moment he felt every ache of those years. He put down the lettuce abruptly and left the storeroom, pushing past Franco.

Antonia moved to follow him but Franco laid a hand on her arm.

"Later," he said. "Get him to come round. I'll stall Tomassino. Make him be reasonable."

After Franco left, Guido dragged a chair outside and sat down to watch the street go by. Antonia was at the cash register, and he could become, once again, the owner of the store.

He sat just under the awnings, squinting out at the sun. A passerby would have seen a short, powerful man, still ruddy in complexion with grizzled grey hair, tight against his skull. But Guido was seeing a younger self, black, tousled hair spattered with dirt, and shoulders that threatened to split his dirty singlet. By squinting his eyes, Guido could see that narrow band of sunlight that his younger self had seen from the bottom of a construction ditch. That small rectangle of light became his sole focus. The fragrance of the flowers and fruit around him was dragged down by the dank smell of clay and sour bodies. He felt cold again.

He looked up. Filippo was standing beside him, his shadow falling over Guido.

"Tomassino's going to throw us out, eh?"

Guido grunted. He was thinking of when Filippo had joined him in the ditches. Sixteen years old and like a bull for work. My God, how they had slaved for the money to get this store.

"Take the deal, papa."

"Go inside, Filippo. I'll handle Tomassino."

Filippo shrugged, his gesture eloquent in describing the foolishness of fighting power with a pop-gun. Guido made no comment. What good was it to tell Filippo that Tomassino had outwitted him? Why try to explain how Guido Vitelli had believed Tomassino's tale of wanting to renovate the block. How he had actually helped persuade some of the older people to sell. But demolition was what Tomassino had been after. Tear down all the old stores, all the years of work and service. Up with fancy new stores at fancy new rents. Yes, thought Guido, he had been slyly trussed up like a goose. A sour taste came into his mouth. Was Franco frying him along with Tomassino?

Guido had three sons. The third was Vincenzo the Babe, the only boy born in Canada. Both his elder brothers had protected him. Filippo, well, Filippo had been like an uncle. And Franco, who was the counsellor and peacemaker for all the neighbourhood gangs, he had protected Vincenzo.

Guido had wished that Vincenzo could stand on his own feet better. All that protection, and all that cosseting from his mother. And then, one day, while he was in high school, Vincenzo announced that he would be going away to take pre-medical courses. Ah, the tears from his mother! Oh, the deep joy inside his father. Vincenzo, another Vitelli, an independent man.

Not, of course, that independent, for there were frequent calls for just a little more money. This Guido paid as he had paid for clothes and car insurance and the odd broken window. The father is the pocket of the family, he had once said. The mother keeps it sewn shut, added Antonia.

That night, Vincenzo called Guido to ask him for money for his plane fare. Guido danced with delight. The boy would be coming home for his sister's wedding. Antonia went upstairs and got his old room ready.

The next morning, Guido drove the old panel truck to the airport to meet Vincenzo. Antonia sat beside him and began craning her neck even before they turned into the tendrils of lanes leading to the terminal.

They parked right in front of the arrival doors and sat there, two old people with expectation written all over them. They were blocking a long limousine from leaving, but the airport policeman left them alone.

Suddenly Vincenzo was in the doorway, long hair brushing his collar, faded jeans tight against his thighs. A girl was with him.

Antonia leaned forward, tense, ready for indignation at a moment's notice. Guido was out of the truck and running towards his son. Vincenzo waved negligently as the girl walked away. Antonia stiffened. The girl's long hair billowed about her shoulders and fell across her eyes. The cleavage of her breasts was apparent and her dark nipples pushed against the thin cotton of her blouse. Like a village whore, the trollop. And my Vincenzo sending her away as though we can't see her, thought Antonia.

The ride back was not as happy as Guido had imagined it would be. But he contained himself and only when he was unloading the truck did he question Vincenzo.

"So many bags. You've got nearly everything with you. Planning to stay for long?"

"A while," was the reply.

The next morning over breakfast, Guido looked at Vincenzo from beneath his lowered eyebrows and said, "Vincenzo. I'm having a sale this week. You'll come and help out."

"Guido!" protested Antonia. "The boy's on holiday. He works hard at school."

"Are you on holiday?" asked Guido.

Vincenzo stared at his plate.

That week Vincenzo worked hard, even Guido had to admit that. Antonia convinced herself that the boy did it as a relaxation from all the studying at school. She came to believe that he was working so hard to prepare himself for the greater mental tasks that lay ahead.

By the end of the week, Guido had great empty spaces on his shelves. Almost all the stock was gone. He announced that they could start clearing the store of its furniture. He wanted to leave nothing for the wreckers. Not even a pane of glass if he could help it.

The decision was made none too soon. The very next morning, a truck arrived with plywood and long lengths of two-by-four. Then the workmen came. They were starting to put the hoardings around Bricetti's Butchers opposite Guido's own Supermarketeria.

"They're starting early," remarked Vincenzo as he came out to join his father on the sidewalk.

"Bricetti's. He's the first to go," said Guido morosely.

"But not without Bricetti," chuckled Vincenzo. "Here comes the old fellow now."

And there was the cadaverous old man himself, tall, gaunt like a crane, and asthmatic in his old age. He watched the workmen with hard, unblinking eyes.

"He's going to give them trouble," said Filippo.

"Naw," said Vincenzo and Guido together.

A workman smashed the glass in the shop window. He had turned too quickly with a long sagging length of pine. "Bricetti" in gold lettering disappeared in long slivers under the feet of the other workmen.

Old Bricetti began to curse the workmen. He began with their allegiance to any country unfortunate enough to shelter them and he moved to the sexual habits of their ancestors. Unfortunately, his asthma kept him from raising his voice, for when he tried to scream, a terrible wheeze would shake his chest and the words would be lost in great, whooping rattles as he fought for breath. So, he stood in the gutter, shaking with rage and making ferocious remarks in a quiet, humming monotone.

The workmen went about their business, paying no attention to him. One of them set up a saw horse and began to saw the long, offensive two-by-fours into shorter sections. This incensed Bricetti who began to find things to throw at the workmen.

"He's going to get to them yet," said Vincenzo.

"Old fool," said Filippo and went inside the store.

Guido said nothing. He was transfixed at the sight of Bricetti. His jaw worked soundlessly.

The workmen laughed at each other self-consciously as they ducked the skittering little missiles that Bricetti tossed their way.

"Pigs," said Vincenzo, not understanding that they weren't laughing at Bricetti.

"Keep out of it," said Guido. He looked up at his own store. "We've got to get my sign down." Vincenzo looked at the long sign with its advertisements for olive oil in the Italian national colours and the proud title "Abruzzo Supermarketeria" between them.

"It's going to be a bitch to get down," he said.

The foreman came out from checking inside Bricetti's old store. A cross-cut of wood spent its last bit of momentum on the door frame as he came out. He went over to old Bricetti and spoke to him.

Bricetti danced with rage and raised his walking-stick to the foreman. The man reached out one massive forearm and knocked the stick away. Bricetti spat at him and the foreman slapped the old man's face, a light, stinging tap as one slaps a child to bring it to its senses.

"Ignoramus!" shouted Vincenzo.

"*Ignoranti*," agreed Guido.

And then to Guido's amazement, Vincenzo bellowed and rushed across the street. The foreman turned to meet him, but a workman stuck out a foot and Vincenzo went flying in mid-charge.

"*Bastardi*," yelled Guido, picked up his chair and rushed forward himself, the chair held like a gladiator's trident in front of him. The men backed off except for one who picked up a two-by-four.

"De Santos," said the foreman in a warning voice.

Guido covered the man with the legs of the chair, never taking his eyes off the man, and said, "Any of you touch my boy, I'll kill the bastard."

"Take it easy, mister," said the foreman. "I already called the cops."

"Did you?" said Guido but his eyes stayed, glittering and hard, on the man with the two-by-four. "Couldn't take the truth, eh? Couldn't take what the old man was telling you. Big man, that's what you are."

"No, mister," said the foreman. "I didn't understand a word he said. I'm Lebanese."

Behind him, Bricetti blighted the Lebanese to the seventh generation. Guido could hear the sirens of the patrol car. Dear God, he thought, now we're in trouble. He wished Antonia had come down to the store that morning.

Bricetti went to pick up a stone.

"Don't," said the foreman. "Please."

The man with the two-by-four took an experimental poke at Guido, who parried with a wild swing of the chair that almost made him lose his footing. The sirens were nearer. Come on, he prayed, come on. This chair is too damned heavy.

Vincenzo had got to his feet. A graze on his arm was bleeding and the workmen looked at him curiously. The patrol car slammed to a halt beside them and the patrolmen got out, briskly.

"Okay. Okay," said one of them. "Let's break it up."

Bricetti wheezed off several remarks about police dictatorship and the misuse of his tax-money. The patrolman gave Guido a slight shove to get him back across the street. Guido set the chair down gratefully and obeyed.

Vincenzo resented being shoved away, but Guido called to him, "Don't look for trouble, son. They're the guys to give it to you."

The foreman ushered his men away except for the one who had kept sawing away during the entire fracas. He caught Guido's eye.

"Hey, mister," he called in a pleasant voice. "What did you do when you first come here? What did you do for work?" He tapped his chest and then pointed at Guido. "Like me, mister like me."

By the end of the week, Guido had cleared out the store. The remnants he could not sell were heaped out on the sidewalk. The big sign was leaning against the storefront.

"That's the last thing to go," said Guido. He looked up at the empty space. Just faintly he could see the old lettering – "Avenue Variety."

"The Sangliaro's owned it," he said to Filippo. "Remember them?"

"All-day suckers, three for two cents," said Filippo. "That's the first English I learned."

Filippo left. There was nothing more for him to do. He was coming over that night. Vincenzo hung around.

"Well," said Guido, rubbing his hands as though he were cold. "We're finished. What are you going to do now?"

"I dunno." Vincenzo looked blank.

"Your grandfather kept my brothers and me on the farm. Know how he did it? We knew he would break our legs if we tried to leave. Sons were money back then. I won't be like that with you boys."

"I understand, papa."

"But don't take too long making up your mind."

Over dinner that night, Guido outlined his plan to start again. Muscillo the jeweller was moving out of his store two blocks away. With the margin he had saved in selling out his own stock plus Tomassino's settlement, he and Filippo could start an even bigger marketeria. He was shaken when Filippo turned him down, explaining that he had got himself a job with one of the big food chains. Constanze smirked at her husband's new-found success.

"A food manager," Guido gasped. "Working for someone else. I'm talking about family, Filippo."

"Someone else?" asked Filippo, his eyes, sly and sleepy. "Family? I'll tell you this. At least there they'll listen to me. I won't be a forty-year-old errand boy," he concluded, his voice rising a surprising octave.

And then everybody started to talk at once and the situation got out of hand. Franco backed Filippo (again confirming Guido's suspicion that they were in league with each other and Tomassino). Vincenzo jumped in, and was called a drop-out by Franco. Antonia closed her eyes tight and Guido lost his temper.

After everyone left, Guido poured himself a large glass of the hated Scotch whisky. A man could get a taste for this, he thought, as he made a face with each sip. Out loud, he said, "I feel like that man, Job, the one that lost his sons and camels. Job, that's what I feel like."

Antonia was scrubbing the dishes within an inch of breakage.

Yes, thought Guido, I have my sorrows now. There's my Angela off among the Bainbridges. They don't listen when we talk to them. They don't even listen to each other. What will my little Angela become? And my sons. Franco helping that Tomassino tear down a life's work. Vincenzo throwing his future away and Filippo not far behind him. He gives up a real future for a little jacket with his name on it. What made them all this way?

"Job had boils," said Antonia.

"What?" said Guido.

"In the Bible. God gave him boils."

"Boils? Ah, what's that compared to my sons?"

"He did it to test him."

"Then I wish He'd tell me what He's testing me for."

Guido had little to do that summer. He thought over the Muscillo deal but he knew that on his own he couldn't make the store go. He had some faint hope that Vincenzo might come in with him. But Vincenzo drifted and they argued and Vincenzo took up with some woman and left home. The house was more silent than ever.

He tended his garden and took walks and wondered what he would do when the garden lay fal-

low and it was too cold to walk. To be at home with Antonia was no longer a pleasure. She'll start wearing black soon, he thought.

Sometimes he went down the old avenue. It was painful but necessary; it kept him alive. One day, down there, he met old Bricetti.

"I thought you were supposed to stay away from here," he said.

"It's gone now," said old Bricetti, looking mournfully at the hoardings. A diesel engine roared and a shovel scraped into the earth and rose, dripping with soil, which it dumped into the waiting trucks.

Guido's store stood empty and eyeless on the other side of the street. Posters flapped on the panels outside.

"What are you doing with yourself?" asked Guido.

"Walk, go to my social club." Bricetti brightened. "You should come over again. You could join now. You're practically a pensioner."

Guido shook his head. He had been to Bricetti's club the year before. It was full of old men. They were a lively lot but old. They even had an exercise cycle that they all took turns riding. They pretended they were doing the Giro d'Italia and they kept meticulous track of how many kilometres they cycled. They cheated a lot. It was amusing, but Guido would want the real Italy, not an exercise bicycle.

Bricetti looked crestfallen. "I guess you got lots going. That Muscillo deal. It's going through?"

"I don't know. He wants to sell before autumn. Lots of sun in the winter at Avenezza. He wants to get away."

"Can't you do it on your own?"

Guido looked at Bricetti. He's thinking of coming in as a partner, but he's too old, too sick. I doubt if he'll last the winter.

"I've got all the help I need. I'm taking my time thinking about it, that's all."

They stood for a moment on that old sidewalk, shuffling their feet awkwardly and then they said goodbye. Guido never saw old Bricetti again.

When he got home, Antonia was cleaning the house. If she wasn't cleaning, she was out visiting the grandchildren. When she was home, she cleaned.

"Did you see anybody today?" asked Guido.

"I didn't go out."

That was a bad sign. Guido threw his hat on a chair and sat down on the couch. Antonia came into the room with the floor polisher.

"Not now," said Guido. "Put it away. Come and sit here."

Leadenly, Antonia came over. Guido stroked her hair.

"*Cara*. Have you ever thought of taking a vacation? Going somewhere?"

Antonia shook her head.

"I've been wondering what the old town is like. Opi. Whether it's still there."

"It's still there." Her eyes wandered over to the cabinet. They had an album of snapshots and postcards in there.

"We could go back – just to see."

"For a vacation."

"Maybe. I don't know. What is there for us here? Back there, with our money, we'd be well-off. Yes, well-off." Guido savoured that for a moment. There could be a big house with a balcony over the street and big walled garden at the back. Many vines and cherry trees. And he would own it all.

"There's our grandchildren," she said.

"They could stay with us. Yes, for their vacations. It would develop their Italian side." Stay with us in the big house, he thought, and learn how to cut vines, crush the grapes. How to care for things.

"Job," she said, twirling one lock of his hair in her fingers. "I thought you were Job."

"Not in Italy," he said.

Guido had learned to leave well enough alone. He left the subject alone until the middle of August. He and Antonia were sitting out in the garden while Franco's children played among the tomato plants and the tall, bobbing corn.

"Next month, I'll be taking all this down," he said.

"You could leave the beans in till October."

"Then, winter. I've never liked winter. Not ever. If we went to Opi. Just for the winter even." And he let the sentence hang.

Antonia gave him a sidelong glance and smiled. She's softening, he thought.

In early September, they had rain. It wiped out the last crop of beans and turned the garden into a banquet hall for slugs. A brown, scaly rot grew on the stems of the plants.

"That's it!" yelled Guido as he came into the house to rinse the mud off. "If it isn't the damn rain, it's the damn frost. You can't grow anything here."

"Franco told you you'd lose your pension going back to Italy now."

"I may not live long enough to draw my pension if I stay here," Guido yelled and he sat heavily at the table. All my strength's been drawn down into my gut, he thought. Look at it. His paunch brushed against the edge of the table as he sat down. It didn't used to do that.

"What have you got against going home? You shouldn't believe everything you read in the papers."

"Ee-eh," Antonia sighed. "It isn't home to me. Everybody will be old like us."

"They're all old here. The Roncari's, Squillaches. We only look young to each other."

"Do whatever you want. In the end, you get your way. You always did."

Now Guido Vitelli had three sons and they had abandoned him. When he booked the tickets for Italy, placed his affairs in the hands of his son the lawyer, and placed scrupulously an exact half of the price he had received from the store into the hands of the food manager, his other son, they both believed that he was abandoning them. Only his third son encouraged him, but that was because he was at loose ends, too.

If we were in Italy, thought Guido, if we had stayed there, my sons would have fought with me, hated me, loved me just like here, but we would have been close. We could not have strayed from each other. But Canada has so many spaces that families get lost in them. I shall become close to them again when my grandchildren visit me.

Every man must pay some price for what he thinks of as freedom. For Guido, it was his grandchildren begging him to stay with them. And their tears were real though he suspected the words had been put there by the parents. And then, his two sons persuaded Antonia that she should let Guido go alone first. He realized that he might stay alone for the rest of his life, but he went anyway.

Of course, after a month or so, Antonia followed him. A lifetime of duty drew her across the ocean to her husband – just as being alone with her two children had led her to him in Canada. They both found Opi unchanged, which delighted them except that they missed the conveniences they had become used to. There was rusty water in the taps, and the plumbing clanked like a mediaeval battle. Antonia settled in, but Guido became a wanderer.

The church had been only the beginning; the ending came in a little café in Opi. There, on a glistening day in spring between the sweet showers that washed the town, Guido went to spend the morning. No one greeted him when he came in. The locals lifted their heads from their games, or papers, or conversation, and went quickly back to their pastimes. Guido had no interest in their talk – politics usually, who was buying whom, whether the mayor would vote the party line – and they had no interest in him and his obsession with a certain Tomassino from Opi who must have had cattle-thieves and German mercenaries among his ancestors. Guido sat alone and ordered his coffee. He squinted his eyes to make the pale sun into a narrow band of light in the street and he could become young again.

On this morning, a stranger came into the café. Guido noticed him and gave a slight nod to indicate that he could sit at his table if he wished. All the other tables were occupied. The stranger sat down. Guido stopped squinting.

"Beautiful day," he said.

"Lovely," said the stranger. "But the highway! All of them driving like they were picking flowers."

"Ah," said Guido, nodding knowingly, although he hadn't driven since the first hair-raising drive from Rome along the *autostrada*.

"I'll be glad to get my feet under my own table, I can tell you."

"Yes," said Guido.

"I'm a salesman," said the stranger, snapping his fingers at the waiter. "My home's about one hundred kilometres away. But my route! Madonna! I'm away for two weeks, often more."

"My home's four thousand kilometres away."

"Ah, you're not from around here. I thought not. Your accent."

Guido frowned. He thought he had remembered the old dialect perfectly.

"American, retired? Yes, I can place your accent. Don't tell me. Chicago."

"Toronto."

"Ah, the second greatest Italian city in the world!"

Guido smiled.

"But you came home to retire." The stranger gave him a keen glance. "Forgive my curiosity. I'm always asking questions. *Market research*, isn't that the English for it?"

Guido yawned elaborately. "Ah, it's a long story. I wouldn't want to bore you."

"Not at all," said the stranger. "I've all the time in the day. You'd be doing me a favour. I want to wait till later for the traffic to clear." He made a little bow with his head. "Tell me how you came to this little town. Go on."

So Guido told him of Angela and the church and how it began. He could not tell whether the stranger listened or not for he became lost in the smells and heats and textures of Toronto. He was surprised at how distinctive it all was and how familiar. And, as he came to the end, he felt a sadness. How could he have wanted to leave his garden? Why hadn't he bought Muscillo's store? He had forgotten how he had exulted all winter in the brisk but never severe breezes of the Abruzzi while he thought of Muscillo in the slush and ice of the Canadian winter.

When he finished, the stranger sat, tipping the sludge in the bottom of the small coffee cup from side to side. He looked quizzically at Guido.

"You intend to stay here?"

"My grandchildren will be coming over for the summer. Part of the summer."

"Ah, and you are happy here. No regrets?"

"You can see for yourself."

"Forgive me. We have an old American in our town. He came back several years ago. I get the feeling that he is not entirely content."

"How can that be?"

"He has told all his stories. Now he has nothing left so he lives on in them. The town ignores him."

"Ah yes. Well, that is his problem."

"That's true."

"He should forget the past. He's in Italy. Not America."

"Yes, it is regrettable. But then, he doesn't realize that America is his home. You see, I travel a great deal. All over the place. And wherever I go, I am a stranger, that's true. At most, a fleeting friend." The stranger smiled shyly as though remembering one warm moment. "But I am not a foreigner. Those people in the buses with sunglasses and cameras, they are foreigners. Now, what if one of them got off that bus and decided, yes, I will stay in Opi. It is a quaint little town. I shall be happy here. What would happen, do you think?"

Guido licked his lips. His throat had gone dry. "Rent a house. Look for one to buy. Settle in, I guess."

"Settle in," said the stranger dryly. "But they have a home elsewhere. What can they offer this town once the quaintness has become familiar? What life do they have?"

Guido looked down at his coffee cup. The stranger looked out on the street.

"Well, I must be going. But, my friend – I can call you that, can't I? My friend, I wish you well. You have given me a most instructive morning."

Guido stood mechanically and partly bowed as the stranger left. He remained standing. He looked around the café intently, memorizing every detail. I must remember all this, he thought, I shall come back here many times, later, many times. But it will be when I am back in my home. Here, I am alienated. The stranger had been right. He had not taken that into account — to be a foreigner where he had been born. And so he left.

He found Antonia gossiping with some women on a sidestreet. They could stand here for hours talking, never moving, he thought. If she stays here, she'll end up in black. She had already stopped wearing the richly coloured knitted hats she brought with her from Canada.

"Come on," he said to Antonia and took her by the arm.

"Let go," she protested when he had led her up the street. "You didn't even let me say goodbye properly."

The town clock struck the hour. It had a

cracked tone, that clock. It had never been the same since that air-raid in 1943.

"Hurry," said Guido. "We'll miss it."

"Miss what?"

He led her up through the narrow streets which became more winding and steeper. They walked together to the top of the town.

"There," he said, pointing out to the swell of the Umbrian hills, purpling in the distance and with the glint of sea beyond them on this clear, limpid day. "What do you see?"

"The mountains. And, I think, yes, the sea."

"Are they beautiful?"

She looked at him in surprise. "Yes," she said slowly.

A little horn blipped in the valley below them.

"What's that down there?" he asked.

"A train," she said, wondering what he was doing.

"The little railcar to Rome," he supplied. "It goes tomorrow morning, too. It's not very pretty but it goes to Rome and there's an airport there."

"So?"

"I'd like you to be on that train tomorrow with me. I'd like you to fly home with me."

"Would you?"

"Yes, with all my heart. I know. I know I never gave you a choice before. But, well," he ended with a shrug. Look at me, he seemed to be saying to her. I'm helpless. "If you want to stay, I'll stay too." He grimaced.

"Guido," she took his arm. "If we stay any longer, we'll both start to rot."

They turned and walked back down into the town. What a woman, thought Guido. She wouldn't have looked good wearing black anyway. Behind them, the little railcar gave a cheeky bleep on its whistle and sped towards Rome.

Epilogue

Today, Canadians can trace their heritages to almost every country in the world. They represent nearly every religion, every race, and hundreds of different cultures. They left their homes in search of freedom from poverty, oppression, persecution, and the strictures of their society. Arriving often penniless and friendless, they sought new opportunities, new adventures, and a new life.

Although Europe has been the origin of most waves of immigration, other countries, flung far and wide, have also provided their share of new Canadians.

The United States was the source not only of United Empire Loyalists, but also black immigrants, the first of whom came to Canada during the American Revolution in 1776 when slaves willing to bear arms were offered their freedom in exchange for joining His Majesty's troops. A second group of black refugees came after the War of 1812. In 1829, the Executive Council of Lower Canada declared that slavery was not recognized by the law of Canada; this decision led to an increase in the number of fugitive slaves seeking refuge in British North America through the dangerous network of the "underground railroad." Over the years a trickle of black immigrants continued to come to Canada even after slavery was ended in the United States. The primary areas of settlement were Nova Scotia and southern Ontario.

From the East came the Chinese and Japanese who were brought to Canada to work on the railroad in the 1800's. Eventually a "head tax" was placed on Chinese immigrants and a strict quota on Japanese immigrants. Canadian immigration laws remained restrictive until 1967. Since then, immigrants have been able to come from Hong Kong, Taiwan, Vietnam, Korea, India, Ceylon, Pakistan, the Caribbean, and from various Latin American nations.

In addition to immigration from many Commonwealth countries, Canada, as a member of the United Nations, frequently receives refugees in large numbers and always accepts refugees in small numbers based on the merits of individual cases. When, for example, homes had to be found for expelled Ugandan Asians, Canada accepted some seven thousand, and more recently has accepted hundreds of Vietnamese "boat people."

Although the experiences of all newcomers have been unique, and the countries and conditions they left diverse, they have all contributed to the vast and encompassing Canadian mosaic.

The Newcomers

inhabiting a new land

A series of seven films
produced for Imperial Oil Limited
on the occasion of the company's 100th birthday
by
Nielsen-Ferns International

Executive Producer	Gordon Hinch
Producers	Richard Nielsen
	Pat Ferns
Associate Producers	Michael Peacock
	Hugh Harlow
Executive Story Consultant	Charles Israel

Series Advisory Board

Donald Avery
Michel Brunet
George Clutesi
Ramsay Cook
Jorgen Dahlie

George MacBeath
John Mannion
Howard Palmer
Antonio Santosuosso
Marcel Trudel

Series Theme
Hagood Hardy
Animated Overture
Directed by Peter Sander
Designed by Danielle Marleau
Animated by Don Stearn

Research Assistants

Barbara Freeze
Anne Girard
Peter Jarrett
Alan Ritchie
Zorianna Hrycenko

Unit and Location Managers

Simon Barber   *Prologue*
Phil McPhedran   *Prologue*
Lyse Lafontaine   *1740, 1832, 1847*
Richard Flower   *1911, 1927, 1978*

Continuity

Clare Walker   *Prologue*
Marie La Haye   *1740, 1832, 1847*
Pauline Harlow   *1911*
Nancy Eagles   *1927, 1978*

Production Managers

Paulle Clark   *Prologue*
Robert Baylis   *1740, 1832, 1847*
Robert Linnell   *1911, 1927, 1978*

Assistant Directors

Bill Corcoran   *Prologue*
Avdé Chiriaeff   *1740*
John Ryan   *1832, 1847*
Gary Flanagan   *1911, 1927, 1978*

Second Assistant Directors

Jacques Hubert   *Prologue*
Avdé Chiriaeff   *1832, 1847*
Don Brough   *1911, 1927*
David MacLeod   *1978*

Production Designers

William McCrow   *1740, 1832, 1847*
Roy Smith   *1911, 1927*

Art Directors

Phil Switzer   *Prologue*
Jocelyn Joly   *1740, 1832, 1847*
Bill Beeton   *1978*

Assistant Art Directors

Alice Switzer   *Prologue*
Susan Longmire   *1911, 1927*

Costume Designers

François Barbeau   *1740, 1832, 1847*
Julie Ganton   *1911, 1927, 1978*

Wardrobe Mistress

Marie-Hélène Gascon   *1740, 1832, 1847*

Construction Manager

Bill Harmon   *1911, 1927, 1978*

Makeup Artists

Phyllis Newman   *Prologue*
Marie-Angèle Protat   *1740, 1832, 1847*
Valli   *1911, 1927*
Shonagh Jabour   *1978*

Property Masters

John Berger   *Prologue*
Ronald Fauteux   *1740, 1832, 1847*
Jac Bradette   *1911, 1927, 1978*

Hair Stylist

James Brown   *1911, 1927, 1978*

Set Dressers

Emmanuel Lépine   *1740, 1832, 1847*
Margot Gascon   *1740, 1847*

Directors of Photography

Albert J. Dunk   *Prologue*
René Verzier   *1740, 1832, 1847*
James B. Kelly   *1911*
Mark Irwin   *1927, 1978*

Film Editors

Eric Wrate   *Prologue, 1847*
Yves Langlois   *1740*
George Appleby   *1832*
Alan Collins   *1911*
Arla Saare   *1927*
Bruce Nyznik   *1978*

Camera Operators
& Assistant Cameramen

Peter Luxford
David Petty
Paul Prince
Denis Gingras
Bill Reeves
Robin Miller

Gaffers

Howie Galbraith
Jean-Paul Houle
Yvon Bénard
John Berrie
Jock Brandis

Grips

Ron Gillham
André Ouellette
Maris Jansons

Boom Operators

Rob Young
Normand Mercier
Jim Thompson

Sound Recordists

Peter Shewchuk   *Prologue, 1911, 1927, 1978*
Ron Seltzer   *1740, 1832, 1847*

Re-Recording

David Appleby   *Prologue, 1740, 1832, 1847, 1911, 1927*
Joe Grimaldi   *1978*

Sound Editors

Eric Wrate   *Prologue*
Jim Hopkins   *1740, 1832, 1847*
Bruce Nyznik   *1911, 1978*
Robert Grieve   *1927*

Second Language Versions

Télé-Montage Inc.

Publicist

Patricia Bowles

Post Production

Paul Quigley
Anne-Marie Jackson
Samuel C. Jephcott
Penny Hozy

Production Accountants

Rosemary Chandler
Cam Cleary
David Copeman

Production Associate

Ellen Adams

Prologue

PRODUCED IN COOPERATION WITH THE 'KSAN ASSOCIATION,
THE PERFORMING ARTS GROUP OF 'KSAN,
AND THE PEOPLE OF HAZELTON, BRITISH COLUMBIA.

THE CAST

Ksaweal	Chester McLean
Sagagwait	David Milton
Neeloak	Tina Hamill
Gallay	Barlow Greene
Kselok	Bob Sebastian
Halaait	Ray Jones
Elders	Ernest Hyzims
	Moses Morrison

Narrator	George Clutesi
	Jean-Paul Nolet
Voice of Ksaweal	Sherman Maness
	Denis Lacroix
Voice of Neeloak	Colleen Loucks
	Catherine Nolet
Special Advisers	Polly Sargent
	Mary Johnson
	Alice Jeffrey
	George Muldoe

Screenplay by Charles Israel
Musical score composed and conducted by Hagood Hardy
Directed by Eric Till

1740

THE CAST

Nicolas de Lugny	Michel Côté
Catherine Gagnon	Louise Lambert
Madame Gagnon	Fernande Giroux
Monsieur Gagnon	Jacques Godin
Officer	Benoit Girard
Intendant Hocquart	Jean Gascon
Nolan	Paul Buissonneau
Elie Cotenoir	Donald Pilon
Pinot La Perle	Yvon Barrette
Dorval	Jean Mathieu
Père Boishébert	Paul Hébert

WITH

Zacharie Bellefleur	Manouck Germain	Guillaume Richard
Raymond Cloutier	Luc Gingras	Omer Rock
Jérôme Décarie	Ronald Guevremont	Tony Roman
Lisette Dufour	Gaetan Lafrance	Ghislain Tremblay
Vincent Fournier	Aubert Pallascio	Gisèle Trépanier
J-Léo Gagnon	Ghislain Picard	Claudie Verdant

Story by Guy Fournier
Screenplay by Claude Fournier
Musical score composed and conducted by André Gagnon
Directed by Claude Fournier

1832

THE CAST

John Symons	Kenneth Welsh
Margaret Symons	Susan Hogan
Nelson	Hugh Webster
Andrew Irwin	Donald Davis
Obadiah Brown	Budd Knapp
Matthew Clark	Neil Shee
Emily Clark	Candace O'Connor
Boyd	Chris Wiggins

WITH

Jessica Burns	Thomas Hauff	Shelagh U'Ren
John Codner	Bernie Lizar	John Wildman
Ian Finlay	Jonathan Ryshpan	Nadia Zacharzuk

AND

Ed Alexander	Thomas Dumbrille	Robert Pye
Marjorie Alexander	Orval Fawcett	Rex Robertson
Guy Barbeau	Peter Glen	Lester Sayer
Jean Barbeau	Dick Grant	Shawn Stone
Pierre Barbeau	Andrew Johnston	Chris Tindall
Garnet Barkley	Howard Jones	Cindy Veenstra
Roy Barkley	Stephanee Lewis	John Worsnop
Toby Bateson	Rick Nielsen	Meghan Worsnop
Wayne Dailey	Gerry Oesterhoo	Peter Wright
	Dennis Palmer	

Screenplay by Timothy Findley
Musical score composed and conducted by Rick Wilkins
Directed by John McGreevey

1847

THE CAST

James	David McIlwraith
Mary	Linda Goranson
Tall Man	Peter MacNeill
Janet	Joanna Noyes
McConnell	Sean McCann
Elsie	Sheena Larkin
Norris	Ken James

WITH

Frank Blanch	Ian D. Clark	Sean Hewitt	Maurice Podbrey
Sara Botsford	Philip Craig	John-Peter Linton	Cornelia Polak
Griffith Brewer	Ita D'Arcy	Walter Massey	Stephen Rosenberg
Patrick Brymer	Desmond Ellis	David McCulley	Deborah Templeton
Wayne Burnett	Charles Foster	Dave Patrick	Bill Vincent

AND

David Bairstow	Dorothy Davis	Jorma Lindquist	John Paul Reymont
Chris Barry	John Dunn-Hill	Kenny MacDowell	Don Robinson
Jim Bearden	Kevin Fenlon	Olive MacRory	Mary Rooney
Tia Blake	Ian Finlay	Jeff Mappin	Noel Ross
Janice Bryan	Basil Fitzgibbon	Thomas McAteer	Nancy Roy
Jacqueline Burns	Marilyn Gardner	Kirk McColl	Jose Ruiz
Carole Carrier	Susan Gibson	Mary McDonnell	Arden Ryshpan
Jeanette Casenave	Sheila Graham	James Messenger	Shauna Sexsmith
John Codner	Vincent Bono Grenier	Denis Moroney	John Shearer
Kevin Conroy	Terry Haig	Mary Morter	Paula Sperdakos
Patricia Conroy	John Heney	Jan Muszynski	Wendy Spingate
Patrick Conroy	Ann King	Robert Parson	Violet Walters
Valda Dalton	Bob King	James Patten	Gordon Warren
Brenda Daly	John King	Philip Pretten	John Wildman
Liam Daly	John Lefebvre	Pauline Rathbone	Roy Witham

Screenplay by Alice Munro

Musical score composed and conducted by Harry Freedman

Jigs and reels by BARDE

Directed by Eric Till

1911

THE CAST

Hollis McLaren
R. H. Thomson
Richard Donat
Fiona Reid
James Hurdle
Barbara Gordon
Mary Pirie

WITH

George Buza
John Friesen
Sean Hewitt
Francesca Mallin
Wally Martin
Marie McCann
Steve Pernie

AND

Jeff Braunstein
Trevor Bruno
Kelly Christian
Karen Cruikshank

Cynthia Grdic
Jefferson Mappin
Tony Moffatt-Lynch
Adam Nielsen
Belinda Pederson

Teddy Pederson
Richard Pierce
Kirsikka Schmalfuss
David Stelmack

Story by Richard Nielsen
Screenplay by Timothy Findley
Musical score composed and conducted by Paul Hoffert
Directed by Eric Till

1927

THE CAST

Old Lypa	Kenneth Pogue
Young Lypa	Duncan Regehr
Nancy	Diane D'Aquila
Hanya	Susan Roman
Dean	E. M. Margolese
Dmitro	Peter Jobin
Marina	Joan Karasevich

WITH

Fred Culik
James Edmond
Trevor Elliot
Mike Ironside
Richard McKenna

AND

Domenic Cuzzocrea	Sharon Noble
Martin Donlevy	Sam Powell
Wally Michaels	Patrick Sinclair
Natalia Mocharuk	Dana Still

Story by George Ryga
Screenplay by Charles Israel
Musical score composed and conducted by Lothar Klein
Directed by René Bonnière

1978

THE CAST

Guido	Bruno Gerussi
Antonia	Martha Henry
Franco	David Calderisi
Filippo	Gino Marrocco

WITH

Ardon Bess
Mary Mancuso
Arch McDonell
Charlotte Odele
A. Pittaluga
Deborah Turnbull
Bob Vinci
Robert Warner
Michael Wincott

AND

Lawrence Benedict	Fabrizio Ifano	Rino Romano
Enzia Berti	Barbara Jacob	Alberta de Rosa
Florence Carenza	Mark Magnatta	Anna Sbrissa
Maria Esposito	George Markos	Henry Specht
Gerardo Esposito	Robin McCulloch	Aldo Vinci
Deborah Fallick	Patricia Nember	Jovan Vujicic
Aaron Ferguson	Anna Pagano	Elias Zarou
Alberto di Giovanni		Janet Zuccarini

Story by David C. Humphreys
Screenplay by Douglas Bowie
Musical score composed and conducted by John Mills-Cockell
Directed by René Bonnière

DESIGN AND PRODUCTION
Frank Newfeld Studio

TYPESETTING
The Coach House Press

COLOUR SEPARATION
Empress Litho Plate

PRINTING
Ashton-Potter Limited (colour)
T.H. Best Printing
Company Limited (text)

BINDING
T.H. Best Printing
Company Limited

JACKET
Herzig Somerville Limited

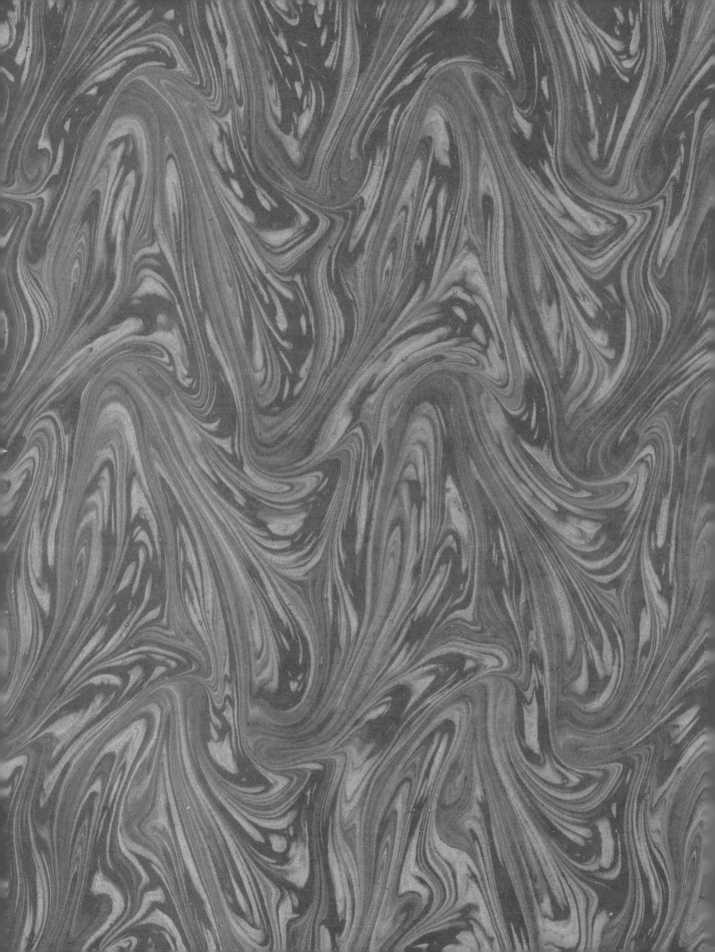